fear the year

Doomsday is coming. The world is about to fall apart.
Devon is the evil genius behind the meltdown. Tristan is
the normal kid whose top secret past holds the key to
stopping Devon. And Genia is the hard-hearted thief
whose fate is caught in the balance.

   Welcome to 2099.

   The end is near.

D1125527

2099

doomsday

2099

doomsday

John Peel

AN
APPLE
PAPERBACK

BOOK 1

SCHOLASTIC INC.
New York Toronto London Auckland Sydney
Mexico City New Delhi Hong Kong

ISBN 0-439-06030-3

12 11 10 9 8 7 6 5 4 3 2   9/9 0 1 2 3 4/0

Printed in the U.S.A.

First Scholastic printing, September 1999

For Charles and Margaret Wetterer

Prologue

Devon stared out at the world with a smile on his lips. It felt exhilarating to be fourteen and to have so much potential. The world was his — his possession, his jewel. . . .

His plaything.

His program was finally ready to run, and he was eager to get started.

"Enlarge," he ordered his computer. "Factor ten."

Obediently, the master mainframe boosted the gain on the hologram. The small globe expanded until it filled the floor below him. Devon grinned again, pleased with the view. He'd been waiting *years* for today. It had been so frustrating, being forced to be patient, when all the while he knew that this fragile globe was his toy. He was looking down on the Americas right now, the most populated portion of the planet. There were almost a billion people living in North and South America — far fewer than, of course, a hundred years earlier, but still a large number for this day and age. He watched as the globe turned slowly, dawn coming to Europe. The start of a new day, which seemed poetic to Devon.

The new day belonged to him. At last he was free to play.

The Doomsday Program was in place, and all it needed was his decision. Then it could begin. But the problem with creating disasters was that they tended to be, on the whole, awfully unimpressive. An earthquake might be fun, for example, but it *might* be taken for a natural event. Devon wanted to show a little more flair.

Blow up a rocket as it launched? There were daily flights to Overlook, which hovered above Earth, and similar runs to the moon and to Syrtis Colony, on Mars. But rockets sometimes exploded on their own, and Devon wanted his mark to be absolutely clear to the world.

That meant doing something that was supposed

to be impossible. The challenge amused him. And, of course, it meant doing something that was bound to be spectacular. Something that would make all the News-bots sit up and pay attention.

A really *great* disaster . . .

And that took imagination. Fortunately, that was one thing he had in great store. He rubbed his hands together.

Party time!

1

"**L**adies and gentlemen, this is your captain speaking."

Sylvie Roth couldn't help grinning at her copilot as she said that. She was still new enough at this business that calling herself *captain* made her glow inside. Matt Bush knew this and winked back at her.

"If you look out of the port windows — that's the left — you should be able to see the skyline of greater London as we head for our landing at Heathrow International Airport. The large towers on the horizon are the Sony Center, of course. Those of you looking for any of the historical sights will, I am afraid, be disappointed for the moment. We're on final approach now, and will be docking in approximately half an hour. I'll be back to tell you more before we arrive." She cut the line and sighed. "I'm never going to get over this thrill, Matt."

"Sure you will," he answered as she walked across to the large window and gazed out at the sea of buildings that was London, ten thousand feet below them. "In . . . oh, fifty or sixty years." He grinned at her.

Sylvie laughed. "Maybe." She walked around the cabin, checking the readouts. Everything, of course, was optimum. If there was the slightest problem, the computer controls would alert her. The *Illysium* was one of the safest craft in the air. And it was all under her command . . . She'd worked hard for this captaincy, and this was her first flight in charge of the airship. It was a day she knew she would never forget, no matter how her career went from here.

Airships were simply the most beautiful things in the sky. Sylvie had loved them as a small girl, and now, as a less-small woman, she still adored them. Some of her friends at flight school had gone into rockets or even aircraft. They had spoken of a love of speed and a desire to push the limits. Sylvie could understand at least a part of that. But she preferred the sedate grace of the airships. Large, slow, and elegant, they moved almost silently through the skies. In a fighter plane, the ground went by so fast you never had the chance to *see* anything. Half of the newer craft were entirely computer-controlled anyway, with the human pilots simply along for the ride. And, Sylvie always thought, if you were riding, then there should be something for you to see.

From an airship, floating along serenely at lower levels, there was *everything* to see. She had crossed over the Grand Canyon, the great Serengeti, the Gobi Desert. And she had seen cities all over the world from the air. There was time to *look*, and to enjoy things in an airship, probably one of the reasons why it was one of the few tourist attractions left in the world. Most people preferred to vacation by hologram — you saw everything without the bother of actually having to pack and leave home — but there were still people who wanted to gently float over the world in complete safety and enjoy looking down on things in person.

It was glorious.

Airships had once ruled the skies at the dawn of aviation, back in the early twentieth century. Then had come the spectacular disaster on the *Hindenburg*, exploding and burning to death over the United States. That had started the decline in airships that wasn't reversed for a hundred years. But now, with the desperate need for speed gone, the airships were back in all their glory.

They were no longer cigar-shaped ships, of course. The *Illysium* was more like a pancake, longer than it was wide. And its skin was no longer fabric, but dura-steel — almost impossible to puncture. The lifting gases were still potentially explosive, of course, but with computer monitoring and absolute control, there was no chance at all of a fire starting. And if, God forbid, one somehow did, the computer backups would have even the slightest spark extinguished in less than a second.

Added to this, airships were *big*. Airplanes tended to be small and cramped, with passengers having very little room even to scratch an itch. They were uncomfortable to sleep in and had meals zapped in tiny kitchens. The *Illysium* had personal cabins, a library, a gourmet restaurant, and plenty of free space to wander. Some ships even had swimming pools, but Sylvie thought that was a trifle tacky. Unlike travel in a plane, a flight on an airship was like staying in a first-class hotel. Little wonder that it was so popular.

Sylvie could see their mooring tower ahead of them now. She adjusted the ship's trim and prepared for descent. The fins moved into position and she tapped the commands to start the compressors. Losing lift was simple enough; the lifting gases were compressed to just the right degree to make them liquid. The loss of lift was gradual, so the passengers wouldn't even notice that they were descending. As always, everything was running absolutely smoothly. Even if it somehow wasn't, they would have plenty of time to correct trouble. Unlike planes, which had only moments if things went wrong, airships sometimes had hours.

"Looking good," Matt announced.

"The ship or me?" she asked, grinning. They had a date later at the hottest spot in town — Disney UK's Hall of Kings. She was looking forward to eating like Henry VIII and tossing the bones to the floor for the animatronic dogs to fight over.

"Both, of course." He grinned back. "I know better than not to compliment my captain. Especially when she —"

Looking shocked, he stopped talking and started to gesture at the controls. At the same second, there was a low-level, two-tone signal. *Trouble.*

Sylvie glanced at the panel. Somehow, the compressors were working too heavily. The airship was starting to descend too fast. Some glitch somewhere . . . She crossed to the panel and tapped in override commands to slow the compressors back down. The floor was starting to tilt slightly under her feet, and that meant that some of the passengers were going to complain to the stewards. That would get her a small reprimand, and ruin an otherwise perfect flight.

The overrides didn't work.

Sylvie stared at the panel, confused. What was wrong here? She cleared the settings and started again.

The older settings, the too-high ones, refused to change. The floor was sloping noticeably now. Glasses would be sliding off tables, and meals into people's laps. *That* would get her into trouble! Matt moved to his set of controls.

"I'm having trouble with the overrides," Sylvie admitted. "Try your panel."

He did so, and then he shook his head. "It's not accepting commands," he replied.

"Blast." Sylvie chewed her lip for a second. "We'll have to dump and reboot the computer. Must be a minor virus or something." Her fingers flew over the panel as she primed the commands and then hit the *initiate* button.

Nothing happened.

She had to hold on to the panel now to avoid sliding away. There were six lights flashing, indicating complaints from the stewards. They could wait. The *Illysium* was descending rapidly.

"This is London Control," came a voice from the air. "Flight 106, you are deviating from your authorized path. Please correct."

"What do you think I'm *trying* to do?" Sylvie answered tersely. "We've got computer problems. The overrides won't work and I can't reboot. I'm going to have to do a manual reboot."

"Understood, 106," London replied. "We'll keep other traffic away from you until you're back to normal."

Good . . . Sylvie smashed her side against the master panel as she tumbled across the room. Wincing, she grabbed hold to steady herself. Then she opened the panel and hit the manual reset. The lights dimmed for a second and then returned. And then died completely.

"We've lost all computers," Matt called, an edge of panic in his voice.

"What?" Sylvie stared at the master panel and saw that he was right: Everything was dead. "That's impossible. I rebooted."

"It didn't work!" he cried, thumping the controls. "It's all frozen. We're locked out! The panel's not working!"

Sylvie desperately hit the reboot again and again.

Nothing was happening. The computer refused to restart.

She straightened up as best she could. The floor was inclined at almost forty degrees now. With no panels operating, Sylvie couldn't tell anything from the readouts. But they were heading down toward London, the compressors having done their work. Like everything else, they had shut down. But the *Illysium* was left with too little lifting gas to sustain them . . .

"Oh, my God . . ." Sylvie whispered. Below them, she could see rows of houses. It didn't look too far down. . . . She tried again and again to unlock the computer or the controls. Nothing worked. . . .

The *Illysium* plunged into the houses. It was traveling at only sixty kilometers per hour when it hit — slow for an airplane, but fast enough. The houses crumpled, crashed, and burned. The airship folded like a concertina, and the durasteel ruptured. The gases ignited, and the whole area went up in a huge, consuming fireball.

Hovering Newsbots, alerted because they'd been monitoring the airport channels, caught the whole thing. The news services sent it out instantly. Several million people saw the *Illysium* disaster on their Screens almost as it happened. They watched either through their terminals or on their wall-mounted viewing Screens as the supposedly safe ship plowed into the houses and exploded.

Death toll estimates started to roll in. Crew of thirty; passenger list of two hundred seventy-nine. Ground casualties . . . at least two hundred. All caught in an inferno and memorialized instantly on videonet.

Devon loved it. Now, the question was — what to do for an encore?

In Buenos Aires, the day was passing as usual. Locals were moving throughout the built-up streets, on their way to work or to shop, or just to visit. Unlike many of the peoples of the world, the Latins hadn't adopted the popular style of staying home and doing almost everything via telepresence. Instead, they preferred to get out of their apartments and houses and physically move about. Thus the city was a tangle of people bent on their own tasks. Had it been New York, it would have looked almost deserted.

Most people traveled by pedway. The moving strips of the pedestrian way lay beside one another, making it a simple matter to enter by stepping onto the slowest, and then moving progressively to the left to the faster lanes. Few cities had such a layout, since most had too few pedestrians to make it worthwhile, but Buenos Aires's pedway was famous and well used. The flits — the small personal transports favored in more northern areas — were less popular, though still used. Some were speeding one or two passengers around the city streets, completely guided by the city's computers, thus eliminating driver errors and accidents.

Normally.

Had anyone been paying attention, they might have noticed that the Newsbots seemed to be thicker in the air than normal. The small flying eyes — each emblazoned with the logo of the broadcast site that operated them — seemed to be gathering around the financial district like the ever-present seagulls that hoped for food.

And then the pedway stopped. Instantly, without warning.

People were thrown, screaming, from their feet, collapsing in piles of injured humanity — at least, those who had been traveling on the slower roads. The ones on the fast lane found themselves traveling onward, minus the pedway, at up to seventy kilometers per hour.

They were thrown like missiles at one another.

Even as the cries of the injured sounded, so, too, did

further catastrophe. The flits all lost their controls at the same second the pedway shut down. Traveling at up to ninety kilometers per hour, these small craft shot in a straight line from where they had been. They collided with one another, or with pedestrians, or with buildings.

It was a scene of utter chaos and horror, and the Newsbots caught every bit of it. The news about the *Illysium* crash had hardly had a chance to sink in with the viewing public before the fresh news broke. Screens switched from the explosions in London to the mass deaths and more explosions in Buenos Aires. Gleefully horrified commentators wondered what was happening in the world, that two such disasters should happen in a single day. Many pointed out that since the Unification, safety had been increasing in the world. They seemed to be almost glad to have some bad news to report for a change. Two major disasters in one day!

"Three," Devon said to himself. "Three's a charm." He'd always liked that silly childhood saying. It was time for his last game. This was more fun than he'd imagined.

The Newsbots, once again, were on the scene to record it. Devon had made certain that they were. They hovered above the small house in the Fairfield subsection of Chicago. It was a pretty normal little housing tract — row upon row of uniform houses, each with their security fences and satellite dishes. Devon's choice was purely chance. That made things more interesting.

Mother, father, and six-year-old son were home when their house "detected" a problem. The fire doors slammed shut, sealing the house completely. Alarms rang, alerting the neighbors to trouble. They poured into the street, wondering what was happening. They saw only a sealed house.

Inside the house, the computer decided the place was ablaze, and that the trapped family had actually escaped. Heedless of their attempts to override the controls, the computer began the sprinklers that would put out the nonexistent fire. Then, since it couldn't detect the fire dying down, it switched on all of the faucets in the house.

The police arrived within fifteen minutes and realized that there was a serious problem. They managed to disable the home security system after it shot one of the policemen, thinking him to be an intruder. As the system smoked and melted, the police attacked the fire doors with axes. It was pointless, of course, because such doors had been constructed to withstand the pressure and extremes of temperature.

Eventually, someone located a rocket launcher and blew open the main door. Water cascaded out. The sprinklers had completely filled the house with water.

Three bodies washed out with the flood.

And, again, the Newsbots caught it all.

Devon had been careful to record all of the news channels. He had his Terminal play the footage back again and again. He watched every tiny detail, from the flames of the airship to the bodies flying through the air in Buenos Aires.

It gave him a warm glow to know that *he* had created this panic, fear, and death. That *he* was in control. That at a word from him, a touch of his finger, catastrophe could strike anywhere in the world that he willed it. It was a good feeling to be in control.

But, slowly, the satisfaction began to fade. The tenth time through, he discovered that he was getting bored. The thrill was dying down. The fun was evaporating. It wouldn't last.

Devon began to understand. The joy was in the *doing*, not in the *knowing*. The glow of satisfaction could only last so long.

Soon, he understood, he would have to begin again.

Perhaps the next time the pleasure would last longer. If not, he would need another fix.

This was always possible. To Devon, *anything* that he imagined was possible.

But now he was hungry. Playtime was over; it was time for dinner.

He turned his back on the replaying death and destruction and went to see what the autochef had made for him today.

2

Tristan Connor watched the party with an air of sophisticated humor — or so he hoped. He wasn't normally a guest at an eight-year-old's birthday party, but
he had been forced to make an exception in this case.
The eight-year-old was Marka Worth, the younger sister
of Tristan's girlfriend, Mora. If it meant making Mora
happy, Tristan was only too glad to be here.

Actually, Tristan liked Marka. She was funny, if a little
rude at times, and full of life. She was in her glory as the
guest of honor, laying down the law about what the other
kids could and couldn't do and when the various foods

should be served. It was amusing, as long as you weren't on the receiving end of one of her withering comments.

Mora smiled at him over the heads of the kids, and he smiled back. He couldn't help smiling — Mora was someone you had to admire. She was almost as tall as Tristan, with short golden-blond hair, slightly Asian eyes (her grandmother had been Korean, when such country names mattered). She looked like a pixie, or some other magical being, and she affected him as though she had true magic.

Tristan caught a glimpse of himself in the window — fourteen years old, slim, almost skinny, with a mass of dark hair. He wanted to think he looked like a poet, but he was afraid that he looked undernourished instead. Some girls (Mora in particular) thought he looked okay. But a poet? He winced. His attempts at writing poetry were all unmitigated disasters.

The closest thing in his life to poetry was the way that Tristan could use a computer. Endlessly fascinated with them, there was little he couldn't persuade them to do for him. Most people simply used theirs as tools, a matter of the same thing, day after day — playing the same old hologames or shopping at the .comstores. But Tristan didn't stay on the predictable paths. He enjoyed exploration, hacking out code and poking around to see what there was. Few people knew how extensive the Net was, or what it really contained. Even fewer could unlock the mysteries of the .comworld. Most weren't interested and never tried.

But Tristan wasn't most people. He was out there, exploring, searching, and finding.

"All right," Marka announced. "It's game time. We'll play Where in the World. Rules are very simple: The Screen will project images for us, and the first person to guess where it is wins that point. At the end of the round, whoever has guessed correctly the most wins a prize. Come on, let's go."

One kid complained that he always lost those sorts of games, but nobody paid him much attention. He trailed along anyway, and for a short while the room was left to Tristan and Mora.

"Enjoying yourself?" she asked him.

"I'm enjoying you," he replied, giving her a hug.

"Sweet," Mora replied, running her gloved hand down his cheek. "I promise, after this we'll go off somewhere quiet together."

"It's quiet here," he murmured.

"For how long? They'll get bored within fifteen minutes, I guarantee it." Mora laughed. "Just enough time to get the presents ready."

"Speaking of which, where are your folks?"

"Good question." Mora glanced up. "Terminal, where are my parents? It won't do for them to miss the best part of the party."

"They are in transit," the Terminal answered in the English accent Mora had programmed it to use. "Time to arrival, ten minutes."

"Good." Mora looked at the table again. "Maybe we should put the presents on the floor? It looks marginally cleaner right now."

Mora and Tristan had barely finished placing the gifts in several neat stacks when the door to the VR room opened, and the kids poured out. The unhappy boy from earlier was looking even more unhappy, and one of the girls was clutching a prize.

"Present time!" Mora announced. Marka beamed at the thought, and immediately grabbed up the first gift, tapping the box to open it. It was one of the newer dolls, which could morph to become a small replica of any of seventeen famous singers. It could then play their songs. Tristan realized he couldn't recognize most of the faces. It seemed as if there was a huge gulf between eight and fourteen! Still, Marka obviously liked it.

And so it went. Marka was in great humor, thanking each child for the gifts and bouncing eagerly on to the next present. She was halfway down the stack when the door chimed and Mr. and Mrs. Worth entered.

"Hi, honey," Mrs. Worth said. "Having a good time?"

"You've missed lots of fun," Marka complained.

"I'm sure we have," Mr. Worth agreed, winking at Tristan over Marka's head. "But we've been getting you a very special present. It's only just arrived, and it's waiting on the roof for you."

"On the roof?" Marka was intrigued. "What is it?"

"Why don't we all go and see?" Mrs. Worth suggested.

Marka abandoned the unopened gifts and led the charge upstairs. Her parents took Tristan and Mora by their arms, laughing, and they followed in the wake.

"They really had one?" Mora asked, almost breathlessly.

"They really did." Mr. Worth cocked his head as they climbed the stairs. "Any second now . . ."

There was a chorus of squealing from above, and he grinned.

"I think she found it," Mrs. Worth said.

The roof of the house was flat and beautifully landscaped. The solar panels on the far end cast a shadow across the lawn. By the flower boxes, the children were all clustered around Marka's present. Mora gasped in delight, and even Tristan couldn't help but admire it.

It was one of the brand-new Pegasus Ponies. Standing just under one meter tall, it was a pure white color. It looked like a miniature horse, except for the two swanlike wings that grew from its shoulders. It seemed to be a little nervous, shying away from eight-year-old fingers that wanted to touch and stroke it. It pulled back on the tether, twitching its wings and kicking up a draft.

"It's *terrific*," Marka pronounced. "Can I ride it?"

"No, honey," Mr. Worth said. "It's not strong enough for that. It has hollow bones, I'm afraid."

Tristan knew this; he'd read up on the Pegasus Pony line when he'd heard from Mora that this was what her parents were buying for her sister's birthday. Mora was actually quite envious; Tristan knew that girls tended to have a thing about horses, even genetically altered ones. The makers of the pony had taken basic horse stock, grafted in genes from swans for the wings, and then maneuvered the genetic blend around to create a genuine flying horse. Of course, to achieve this they had been forced to make some compromises. Horses are normally very solid animals, and there was simply no way a pair of wings could get one off the ground. So the manufacturers had hollowed out the animal's bones and reduced its size. The creature also had a mass of muscles behind the shoulder to power the wings, giving it a bit of a hump-backed appearance. This didn't seem to put the kids off, though.

"But it *can* fly, can't it?" Marka asked, looking worried.

"Oh, yes," her father replied. "Guaranteed. You can play with it, and walk it without any trouble. But no trying to ride the poor thing. You'd break its back, even though you're so light."

Marka nodded her understanding. She stroked the pony, which whinnied in apprehension. Apparently it wasn't used to being the center of so much attention. Tristan couldn't blame it for being nervous. The kids were petting and stroking it. Then one hand accidentally poked the pony's eye. It gave a cry of pain and fear and reared back, hooves kicking. The kids moved away, but one boy tripped over the rope tethering the pony.

The pony gave a cry, jerking back — and the rope snapped. With a powerful beat of its wings, the pony tried to leap into the air. Mr. Worth gave a cry and jumped for the rope. The pony didn't have room to actually get into the air, but it panicked and bolted toward the edge of the roof. There was a three-meter fence around it to prevent anyone accidentally falling over, but Tristan knew the pony could leap it without a problem. If the pony had enough momentum, it could fly away. If it didn't, it would fall, and the impact with the ground two floors below would undoubtedly break every bone in its fragile body. Either way, a disaster.

Tristan sprinted after the horse, thankful for his own long legs. The pony had reared up to leap when Tristan's questing fingers closed on the rope and he collided with the fence. The impact winded him, but he kept hold of the rope. Then Tristan wound the rope around the fence, climbing up to tie it as high as possible. As he was doing so, the pony, still panicking, kicked out.

The hoof was lighter than that of a normal horse, so it didn't crack Tristan's skull. Instead, it just bruised him — but the impact made him lose his balance. With a cry of pain, he toppled backward off the fence.

Mora fought back tears as she watched Tristan being loaded carefully into the ambulance. The terrifyingly large pool of blood from where he had hit the ground was being burned by a Technie, methodically eliminating all traces of it.

"Will he be all right?" she demanded of the ambulance attendant, who was locking the doors on Tristan now.

"He's got a fighting chance," the man replied. "A couple of broken bones, a slightly fractured skull. Lost a bit of blood, but that can be made up." He smiled, and patted her cheeks with his gloved hand. "He's young, and he's got you to look forward to. I'm sure he'll be fine. But I have to go now. Check with the hospital in an hour."

Mora nodded bleakly. She watched as the Technie finished his work — he'd been fast but thorough, leaving behind no traces of Tristan's blood — and then clambered into the ambulance. Lights pulsing, it raced away. She was anxious, wondering if the attendant had been correct, or whether he'd just been lying to make her feel better.

Her father put a gentle arm about her. "He'll be fine," he promised, though he couldn't possibly be sure of the fact. "We'll call the hospital as soon as we can."

Mora nodded, and allowed herself to be led back into their house. The physical guests were all leaving now, both of them. The others had cut their link to the house, returning to their own VRs. The party was truly over now.

Marka touched her sister. "I'm sorry," she said, sincerely.

"I know." Mora tried to smile for the sake of her sister. "I'm sure he'll be okay," she lied. She wished she could believe this. But there was nothing that she could do or know for at least an hour.

Tristan would be okay.

He *had* to be.

Taki Shimoda sat quietly beside her boss, trying not to be intimidated by the people in the room. It looked like a simple board meeting of any company, but it was far, far more than that. This was the board of Computer Control, and the twenty-four people who sat in this room — either actually here or, more likely, projections — effectively ruled the world. Politicians might think that they held the power, but since Control ran the Net, and the Net ran the world, *this* was the center of power for the entire planet.

Shimoda might have been flattered and a little awed to be here if it wasn't for the fact that she was likely to annoy them with her report. If she handled it badly, she would be out of a job and, possibly, out of any future jobs.

Her boss was Peter Chen, the head of Net Security, and he was taking a lot of anger from his fellow board members. In the background, footage of the *Illysium* disaster played over and over.

"Our public image is under attack," Luther Schein

said. Shimoda's hand-comp informed her that he was head of customer relations. He waved at the pictures. "This is very bad for us."

It was worse for the victims, Taki thought, keeping her face inscrutable.

"I understand that," Chen replied, striving to keep his temper steady. "But we had no warning that anything was to happen."

"And yet the Newsbots were there," Anita Horesh said crossly. The hand-comp said this was the head of development.

"Yes," agreed Chen. "They were. Someone alerted them approximately five minutes before each disaster."

"Then surely," Martin van Dreelen murmured, "you have at least one person on our payroll who is competent to trace such an alert?" A murmur from the vice president was worse than the bellowing of everyone else. Shimoda's throat went dry, knowing that most eyes had turned to stare at her.

"Normally, yes," Chen admitted. "If you please, Inspector Shimoda will make her report to the board now."

This was it . . . Shimoda stood up and stared directly across the table at the vice president. As long as he understood, it didn't really matter about the rest of them.

"The feeds to the Newsbots were encrypted in a very unusual fashion," she reported. "I managed to break the encryption, but it did not lead to a site. It led only to a name: *Quietus*. I could not penetrate beyond that."

"Quietus?" Horesh scowled. "What is that? A person? A company?"

"We do not know," Shimoda admitted. "There are no subscribers with that name. It may be either a person or a group. Either way, there are no traces of it or them on the Net."

"You are sure this is not simply incompetence on your part?" van Dreelen growled, glaring at her in direct challenge.

Shimoda swallowed and attempted to look completely confident. "I am certain. Normally, I can trace *anything*. But this is beyond my skills — at the moment."

"Are they a terrorist group?" Schein asked. Several members of the board leaned forward at this question.

"I do not think so," Shimoda replied. "It does not act like one. There have been no statements by anyone claiming responsibility, and no demands of any kind. Terrorists invariably want something and are only too happy to let you know what it is and why they should have it. Generally with a political statement for the broadcast sites. In this case, there was nothing of that sort."

"Why would anyone do something like this?" demanded Miriam Rodriguez, gesturing at the exploding airship.

"Probably because they *can*," Shimoda explained. "And they wish us to know that they can. The airship's black box survived the crash, naturally. I ran diagnostics on the *Illysium*'s systems. They show that everything was functioning normally until several minutes before the crash. Then a virus infected the system. It changed all of the command codes, locking out the captain. She reasonably attempted to reboot and regain control. The virus then wiped the system clean, and the computer could not come back on-line. I attempted to backtrack the virus, but this was not possible. And when it destroyed the computer core, the virus self-destructed. There was nothing left of it."

Using the hand-comp, she changed the video feed to the Buenos Aires disaster. "In the second case, computer control of the pedway was infected and shut down."

"Aren't there safeguards against such a thing?" demanded Horesh.

"Yes," Shimoda admitted. "They were all nullified by

the virus. They were so badly damaged that they are still off-line now and undergoing massive systems repair. No virus that we know of could manage such a thing."

"Then this is clearly one we *don't* know of," snapped Schein.

"Exactly," Shimoda agreed. "And it is of such complexity that the Net is completely vulnerable."

There was absolute silence at this shocking statement. Shimoda blushed, feeling the eyes of everyone locked on her face.

"Are you telling us," van Dreelen finally said, "that whoever did this could strike anywhere and at any time and nobody working for us could stop them?"

"Yes." There. It was out. The terrible truth.

The devastating possibility.

The vice president nodded. "I assume you haven't come here just to hand in your resignation," he said softly. Looking around the table, he added, "Though I am sure there are several people here who might be inclined to demand it. Do you have anything positive to offer us?"

"Two things," Shimoda said. This was the moment of truth. "First of all, we do know that we are looking for a person or group known as Quietus. Second of all, I have a program already running that will alert me if the name is invoked again. Whoever killed all of these people wants publicity. He, she, or they will strike again. Once the Newsbots are alerted, I will be prepared to track the virus."

Van Dreelen considered. Shimoda held her breath, knowing his decision could make or break her life. Finally, he gave a curt nod. "It sounds reasonable to me." He glared around the table, as if daring anyone to disagree with him. "I suggest that you get back to work, Inspector. I'm sure Mr. Chen will alert us if you make any breakthroughs."

Shimoda nodded, bowing slightly to cover the rush of emotions to her face. She was incredibly relieved. Of course, this was only a reprieve. If she failed to carry through her plans, then the board might decide to remove her anyway. She had only until their next meeting to prove herself.

And, she vowed, she would have Quietus — whoever or whatever it might be.

Devon called out, "Halt!" and the computer froze the image of the board meeting. He sighed. The first time he'd been able to watch Control's meetings, he'd experienced an electric thrill. They were, after all, his greatest foe, even if they didn't know of his existence. Watching them, knowing they were ignorant of him, had seemed like such great power.

Then.

But after watching months of their futile meetings, Devon had changed his mind. They might be the most powerful people in the world, but they were really just a bunch of boring jerks who employed other people to do the real work. They were *dull*. All they did was talk, and only varied *that* when they argued. And it was adult arguing, which meant that it was mostly acidic and polite. Nobody really insulted anyone else, or cursed them out or anything. It was relentlessly, boringly polite.

This was what power brought you? Ha! They didn't deserve it. And they wouldn't keep it for very much longer.

After all, they didn't do anything *interesting* with their power. They never destroyed cities, or wrecked people's lives, or anything worthwhile. No, they sat around and *talked*. It was like a twenty-four-hour-a-day sleep site, guaranteed to send you yawning to bed. They didn't understand how to play The Game properly. They let little things like laws get in the way. They didn't understand that when you played The Game, *you* made the laws.

But there was one small possibility for fun here.

Devon walked into the frozen hologram and stared into the face of Inspector Shimoda. *This* one had possibilities. Sure, she was a police officer, which meant that she'd stick to the rules. But the fire in her eyes suggested she'd be fun to play with. And she had come up with a couple of good ideas.

If she was dealing with the normal sort of player, she might even stand a chance of winning.

But she didn't have a prayer of catching him. Devon grinned. Unless, of course, he led her on . . . It might be fun to make her think that she was getting somewhere, only to smack her down at the last minute.

Devon grinned wider. Let her play The Game if she wanted.

She would definitely lose.

3

ristan awoke, feeling rather numb. For a moment he wondered what had happened to him. Then he remembered falling from the roof, and the ground coming up to hit him hard. He was amazed he wasn't in more pain until he saw the drip attached to his arm. He looked around and saw a pretty woman smiling sympathetically down at him.

"I'm Dr. Morton," she said. "How are you feeling?"

"Numb," Tristan mumbled. His mouth felt frozen.

"I'm not surprised," she answered. "We've got you on tranks. I'm glad to see you're back with us."

"How am I?" he asked her.

"Not bad, considering you apparently thought you could fly." Dr. Morton looked more serious now. "Slight concussion, and a small fracture at the back of your skull. It'll be simple to grow it back and close up. No brain damage, even if you do feel fuzzy. And a lot of bruises. Oddly enough, your main problem is that you lost a lot of blood. That's one of the other reasons you're feeling light-headed. Now, we've got a sample out for replication, and we'll have a supply for you in a couple of hours. It figures you'd have a rare type, right? Anyway, both of your parents are on the way, and one of them should be a match for you, so we can get a blood transfusion to hold you over." She smiled encouragingly. "And there's been this really cute girl calling to ask how you are. Mora, I think her name is. Is she your girlfriend?"

"Yes." Tristan felt better knowing Mora was worried about him.

"You're a lucky guy then. Now, is there anything I should know about your medical history that would help me treat you? Any allergies, that kind of thing?"

"Allergies?" Tristan asked, not knowing what she was talking about.

"I guess not then." The doctor smiled. "Once in a

very long while we get a rare case of allergies, even though most people had them fixed before they were born. So I have to ask, just for the record. So you don't have any?"

"Not that I know of." Tristan was getting kind of fuzzy again.

"Okay." Dr. Morton leaned forward. Tristan could smell the slight touch of perfume in her hair. "I'm going to let you go back to sleep; it'll help your body to heal faster, and there's not a lot you can do right now anyway. When you wake up again, I promise you'll feel a lot better. Especially if that Mora gets visiting hours right." Her smile was the last thing that Tristan saw for a while.

Panting hard, Genia flattened herself against the wall and listened carefully. There was the sound of running feet, but they were heading in the other direction. It looked like she'd been able to lose her pursuers after all. Still, it didn't hurt to be careful. She stayed where she was, lost in the shadows, and listened until all she could hear was her own heart beating. Then she decided that it was safe to move on.

Now she had even less time to work — she'd have to move fast. She hefted the chip she held and grinned. The man she'd "accidentally" stumbled into probably wouldn't realize that there was anything wrong for a while. And she doubted that the shield who'd been chasing her knew exactly what it was she'd done — he probably thought she'd picked the victim's pocket or something. That was the good thing about shields — they had no imagination.

Genia slipped through the shadowed streets. It was still early afternoon, but very little light seeped down from Above into the Underworld. The buildings here were old and not in the best of repair. The building commissioners for New York ignored this place. They simply demolished houses and buildings from time to time, driving huge new piers into the ground to support the fancy, expensive buildings of Above. The rest of the blocks were simply left to rot, with the castoffs of society living there as long as they could.

Genia had lived longer than most, simply because she was brighter than most. Her folks had once lived Above, but the stock market cataclysm of 2083 had thrown them out of work a few months before she was born. Her father had tried to embezzle enough money to keep them afloat, but he'd botched his coding and was caught. Genia's mother had been ejected into the Underworld; anyone connected with criminals was treated as if he or she had some awful, infectious disease. In such terrible conditions, Genia had been born. Her mother had been able to look after her somehow until Genia was seven. Then she'd been killed by a Cloud. There were no Cloud Alerts down in the Underworld; the people in charge were glad when anyone down here died.

Genia had been forced to strike out on her own. She'd had no other choice except to die as well, and Genia always told people that dying was the last thing she wanted to do. Her mother had taught her coding, and Genia was a natural at it. She'd outdistanced her mother's skills by the time she reached her sixth birthday. Now she was one of the best hackers in the world. She could do what nobody else — as far as she knew — could.

Genia had invented a small scanner that was now attached to her arm, under her coat. It contained a blank chip. All she had to do was to run the scanner across any legitimate chip and she could copy the coding. Then her fake chip would do anything the original could do. It was ludicrously simple. All she needed was a terminal to log into, and she could steal her victim blind before he even knew she'd taken anything. Then she'd blank out the chip and select her next victim.

It had never failed her.

There were lurkers in the streets, of course, but most of them knew her by now. None of them was dumb enough to attack her. Not anymore. She was only sixteen, and skinny, but she worked out and every ounce of body weight was essential. She was all muscle and reflex. She carried a sharp knife up her sleeve and a tazer in the top of her boot. The lurkers stayed to themselves, leaving her alone.

She made her way through the decaying buildings. It was almost instinctive because over the years she had memorized all of the dark, decimated passages. There were access points to Above all over, of course. And, naturally, there were no public Terminals in the Underworld. She'd have to go up again to use her stolen chip. And she'd have to look like she had every right to do so. She dressed nicely but not too flashily — tight yellow jeans, a silver top, and a bandetta holding her long deep-black hair in place. She knew she really ought to cut her hair shorter, to fit in better, but she couldn't help it. It was her one vanity, and she hesitated to allow anyone to touch it.

Of course, she didn't *need* to have short hair, like those who lived above. *They* had to be constantly afraid that someone would steal some of their DNA — be it hair, blood, or skin cells — to use illegally. She didn't have an Implant Chip — an IC — and never had. Unlike the privileged classes who lived Above, she hadn't undergone the insertion of the chip as a child.

As far as the Net was concerned, she didn't exist. Which meant that nobody could find her if she didn't want to be found. To the watching eyes and electronic ears up Above, she was the invisible girl. They couldn't track her, and they couldn't find her. They couldn't even track the chip she'd created until she activated it. It was only when she took it past a sensor that Control would realize her victim was apparently in two places at once. Then the shields would start a sweep.

As if she was dumb enough to allow that to happen.

She reached the ladder that she was heading for, gripped the rungs, and clambered up. As she did, she heard a strange sound off in the distance. A roaring noise, like the drains made after a storm. But there hadn't been one today. The roar was joined by a low, growling kind of sound. Then a far-off scream.

Genia's skin tingled with fear. She was sure the Tabat had to be near. Everyone she'd ever mentioned it to had laughed at her, accusing her of being foolish, credulous, or just plain stupid. But *something* killed the dwellers in the Underworld without warning, leaving only shreds of skin and broken bones behind. Most people claimed it was simply gang warfare, but Genia was sure they were wrong.

There was some kind of a monster that prowled the streets of the Underworld, killing when it got hungry, devouring its unlucky victims. Genia was determined never to be one of them.

Hurriedly, she pushed up on the access hatch above her head and slipped through it into the broom closet where the Cleaningbots hid until they were needed. This was a great place to slip into and out of Above because there were few people around, and no monitoring. The 'bots, of course, didn't count. They simply moved to avoid her and otherwise completely ignored her existence. Which was just how she liked it.

Plus, there was a bank close by.

She moved out of the closet, down the hallway, and into the foyer of the building. There she mingled with the dozen or so people leaving the office, and went out into the streets with them. She always found this amusing. If any of these people knew she was from the Underworld, they'd be horrified of her — they'd move away, afraid they'd catch some terrible disease. But because she looked and acted like them, they believed she was as good as they were.

Genia knew she was *better* than they were. They

were the lambs; she was the wolf that hunted them, un-
suspected.

The streets were almost empty, of course, and Genia
crossed to the bank. She waited in turn for a Terminal,
watching the man ahead of her. She had no idea why he
was out walking — most people made their Terminal
transactions from home. Maybe he just liked the exer-
cise. Maybe he was meeting someone. It didn't matter
to her. She was just awaiting her turn.

"Place your arm to the scanner," the Terminal instructed the man pleasantly. He obeyed, placing his left
wrist over the small panel. The Terminal scanned the
arm, connecting to the IC under his skin and reading all
of the information. It established his identity in less
than a second, then brought up his accounts and personal data.

"Please donate a sample of skin," the Terminal requested.

The man drew back his glove, exposing his bare skin.
He tapped one finger against the sample area, and
the Terminal extracted a few cells. This was the beauty
of the system, its creators believed: To access an account, you needed not only the information on the Implant Chip, but also a pure DNA sample. The Terminal
matched both together before allowing anyone access.

"Please continue with your business," the Terminal said. The man worked for a moment or two longer, and then pressed to end. The Terminal destroyed the skin sample and wiped the account code from its memory. This was to prevent thieves from simply reusing the man's information.

As if! Genia thought, grinning to herself. *That would be too easy.*

The man left, giving her a brief glance. Genia knew she looked good, so she flashed him a cheeky smile back and stepped into the Terminal cubicle.

"Place your arm to the scanner," the voice instructed her. Genia slid the chip into place in her device and pressed her information-thief to the panel. The Terminal scanned the stolen information.

"Please donate a sample of skin," the voice requested.

Genia pulled back her glove and scraped under her index fingernail. When she'd bumped her victim, she'd scored her fingernail lightly across the back of his neck. He'd most likely assumed he'd been bitten by an insect.

The flakes of skin she'd scratched were read by the computer.

"Please continue with your business," the Terminal

said after a moment, fooled as always. Genia grinned and started to work. She brought up the man's whole life and net worth. He was reasonably wealthy, which meant she could siphon off a nice sum before he was likely to miss it. She wasn't interested in anything else. She paid for a hotel room at the Disney Colony, since she hadn't used that place for a while, and ordered food and drink to be there when she arrived. Then she did a little shopping, buying the electronic parts she always needed and a few new items of clothing. Her next purchase was an order of books from a specialty .com store. Despite being a computer genius, Genia liked to actually hold a book and read it, rather than scan one on a screen. It felt much better.

A few little extras: some new music she'd been wanting and some food supplies. That would be as much as she could carry around without raising suspicions. A few keystrokes and Mr. Rikard Lytton paid for her purchases. Genia then tapped into the Terminal's control coding and gained access to the cubicle monitor. She erased the images for the few minutes she'd been there, set the clock back by those minutes, and then downloaded a virus that would take the Terminal off-line in an hour or so for repairs, to explain away the missing minutes.

Nobody knew she'd been here, and there was absolutely no way to trace her. Genia finished the transaction and left the Terminal. She gave the elderly woman waiting to use it a nice smile and hurried off to a lovely meal at the Colony.

It had been a good day's shopping.

When Tristan woke again, he was feeling considerably better. The dizziness was quite gone and he felt tired, but not at all sore. He blinked a few times and saw that the room was much the same as before. Except that instead of Dr. Morton, Mora was sitting by his bed, watching him anxiously. When she saw that he was awake, she leaned forward and took his hand, smiling hopefully.

"How are you feeling?" she asked.

"Hey, waking up to see you?" he managed to joke. "How could I feel less than perfect?"

"Idiot." But she smiled genuinely this time. "Do you really feel better?"

"Yes," Tristan said honestly. "The fuzziness is gone, and so is most of the pain. Just a few sore spots, probably where I'm a mass of bruises." He squeezed her hand. "How is everyone else? Not feeling too bad about the accident, I hope?"

"Well, Mom is still a nervous wreck," Mora admitted. "She's convinced that it was all her fault, somehow. You know how she can get. And Dad . . ." She sighed. "I think he's more worried that you'll file an InstaSuit for damages than he is about you being injured. He's talking to the insurance company about paying you off before you ask."

That was rather typical of her father, but it hurt Tristan to be so mistrusted. "I'm not going to InstaSue him," he grunted. "It was just a dumb accident."

Mora kissed his forehead. "Don't tell him that; let him suffer. He deserves it. Anyway, the Pegasus has settled down now, without all the kids around. He and Marka are getting along really well."

"Good." Tristan managed a weak smile. "Are my folks around?"

"They took a break while I was here. They're getting something to eat. They've been here forever."

Tristan frowned. "How long have I been here?" He couldn't tell, but it seemed like just a couple of hours.

"Well, we've just started day two," Mora answered. "So, about twenty-six hours."

"It doesn't seem that long," Tristan confessed. "Mind you, I've been able to sleep for most of the time. I guess that's more than you or they have."

"We all got a little," Mora said. She looked worried. "Why? Do I have bags under my eyes? Are they red?"

"You look as beautiful as ever," Tristan assured her. "Anyway, speaking of food, I'm getting kind of hungry. Do you think they'll let me eat?"

"Wait here. I'll go fetch the doctor and ask her." Mora squeezed his hand again and then left the room.

Tristan felt a little drained and definitely hungry. Other than that, he realized he had been very lucky. He could have damaged something that would have taken longer than a day to regrow. He could have even been killed. Some forms of broken necks, he knew, were still fatal. It was amazing that he'd suffered so little, really. It was all his own fault for being so clumsy and thoughtless. But he had to admit that he liked the thought of Mr. Worth trying to settle a nonexistent lawsuit. He liked Mora's father, but the man was way too obsessed with money.

That was why he'd bought Marka the Pegasus Pony: It was a status symbol, showing that he could afford to purchase such gifts for his children. He wanted everyone to know how well-off he was. Tristan was always amazed that Mora had turned out so well, considering what a snob her father was. He remembered when he'd started to date Mora, Mr. Worth ran a complete background IC check on him to make certain the boy was in the right sort of class to be dating his treasure! Luckily, Tristan's father was a vice president of a bank, and that was acceptable to Mr. Worth.

The door opened again, and Mora returned with Dr. Morton. The woman looked as fresh and cheerful as he remembered, so she must have found time to sleep, too. She came over and checked the readouts on the panel at the foot of his bed.

"Well, everything's looking good," the doctor said. "How are you feeling?"

"Good enough to be hungry," Tristan replied.

Dr. Morton laughed. "Ah, that's an excellent sign! If you're desperate for hospital food, then you *must* be getting better. I'll have something sent up to you very shortly." She paused to make a note on her wrist-comp. "You're making excellent progress, and I don't see why you can't go home tomorrow. As long as you take it easy for a day or so, you should be playing football again in no time. Of course, you'd be doing even better if you hadn't forgotten to tell me you were adopted."

"Huh?" Tristan wasn't sure he'd heard her correctly. "I'm *what*?"

"Adopted." Dr. Morton frowned. "I should have known better than to ask while you were on tranks, I suppose. But it was obvious when I ran the DNA work on your folks to see if they could donate blood. It didn't match yours at all."

"What?" Tristan was starting to panic now. "What are you talking about? I'm not adopted!"

Dr. Morton stared at him. "You mean you didn't know?" she asked slowly. "They never told you?" She rolled her eyes. "Look, I'm sorry. I seem to have unwittingly broken a family secret. But there really is no doubt; your parents are not your biological parents."

Tristan stared at her in shock. He could hardly believe what he was hearing, and yet she seemed to be absolutely sure of herself.

Adopted? Why had he never been told? He felt as if his whole understanding of the world was crumbling to pieces.

What was going on?

4

Mora quickly went to find Tristan's parents and bring them back. He had to talk to them.

Adopted . . .

Why had they never mentioned this? Why hadn't they ever told him the truth? If he couldn't trust them on this — then what *could* he trust them on?

For as long as Tristan could remember, his parents had always taught him to do the right thing. They had quietly but firmly instilled in him a love of decency, and he had learned to do good — even when it was the unpopular choice — and always to tell the truth.

Always . . .

And yet — here he was, sitting in a hospital bed, and he'd been hit with the biggest lie of them all. His parents had lied to him all of his life. Maybe when he had been a kid he wouldn't have understood. But he was old enough now! *Why* had they lied to him, breaking everything they had taught and expected of him?

His mind was in a turmoil worse than his body had been. He simply couldn't get past the single point; his mind kept insisting on returning to it. He had always believed he knew who he was. But now he didn't.

If he wasn't his parents' son, then who was he?

The door opened, and Mora and his parents came in. His father closed the door slowly and turned to face the bed.

"Is it true?" Tristan blurted out. It wasn't the question he wanted to ask, but he had to hear them admit it.

"Yes," his mother replied, so quietly he hardly heard.

Tristan trembled. It was what he had feared and dreaded. "Why didn't you ever *tell* me?" he demanded.

His father sat on the bed and swallowed hard. "We . . . we were asked not to, when you were given to us," he answered. "Unless you found out for yourself. We promised."

This wasn't making any sense to him. "But *why*?" he cried.

"Since you now know," his mother said, "I think we're free to tell you the rest." She laid a hand on his father's shoulder and squeezed supportively. "Go ahead."

Tristan stared at his father, waiting.

"When your mother was in the hospital," his father said slowly, "there were several complications. The child was born . . . dead. There was nothing anyone could do. We were reconciled to our loss when one of the doctors came to us. He told us there had been a second baby born in the hospital, and that it had been abandoned. It could all go through legal channels, he explained, which would leave the baby — you — in limbo and in need of comfort for days, or even weeks. Or he could alter the records to show that the baby was our child, and the dead baby was the one that had to be given up.

"Maybe we shouldn't have done it, but we were desperate for a child. So we agreed. We needed a child to love, and you needed parents. It seemed like a wonderful arrangement. The doctor made us promise never to tell you that you were adopted. He said it was for your own safety. People *had* to believe that you were our child."

"My safety?" Tristan was startled. "What did he mean by that?"

"I don't know," his father replied. "He just stressed that it was absolutely essential that everyone — especially you — believed that you were our birth child. Otherwise there would be danger. And then he said that if you ever discovered the truth, or if *anyone* did, then we should tell you what we knew."

"Which isn't much," his mother added. "Just that his name was Dr. Taru. He wouldn't say very much else."

"Only that you were to watch out for someone or something called Quietus."

"Quietus?" Tristan didn't understand any of this. "What is it? Or who is it?"

"I've no idea," his father admitted. "I've tried searching for any .comrecords with that name over the years, but there's nothing at all on the Net. We don't have anything else that we can tell you."

His mother patted his hand. "Except, of course, that we love you. We've always felt that you were our child, Tristan, and we've never regretted what we've done. Can you forgive us?"

Tristan considered the question. "I don't know," he said quietly. "I'm going to have to think about this for a while. It's all an incredible shock to me."

His father nodded and stood up. "We'll leave you to think about it," he said. "It'll probably be easier without us around." He took his wife's arm. "Come on."

When they were gone, Mora looked down at him. "Poor Tristan," she said gently. "Do you want me to go, too?"

"Not right away," he answered. "I need somebody here right now who I know I can trust." He sat up and hugged her tightly. "Mora, I feel so betrayed."

"Your parents did what they thought was right," she said carefully.

"I know that. But they should have *told* me, not left me to discover it for myself, like this. I don't care what they promised. They always taught me to tell the truth. But they couldn't bring themselves to be truthful with me." Mora didn't say anything; she just hugged him back. That contact meant a lot to him — he felt as if he was somehow taking strength from her. He couldn't imagine what his life might be like without her. She was the one person in the world he could depend on utterly.

After a few moments, he let her go. "We have to get busy," he said, making a decision. "According to Dad, this Dr. Taru said I might be in danger if I found out who I was. I don't know why he may have thought this, but I have to assume he knew what he was saying. I'd better not stay here any longer. You'd better find me Dr. Morton, so I can get discharged."

Mora looked alarmed. "You really think you might be in danger?"

"I don't know *what* to think anymore," Tristan said bitterly. "I don't even know who I am any longer. But I'd have to be a total idiot not to take that warning seriously until I find out more."

"I know who you are," Mora replied gently. She smiled at him. "You're someone who wants to climb waterfalls, and not just watch them on a Screen. You're someone who can't lie to anyone without blushing. You're someone who risks his neck to save an eight-year-old's birthday. And you're my boyfriend. Whoever else you are doesn't much matter to me. You're still Tristan, the same wonderful person you were an hour ago."

"Thanks." He felt better with her support, but it wasn't enough. "We'd better get moving, just to be on the safe side." Mora nodded and left.

Was he overreacting? Possibly. But it was safer than not taking things seriously. The idea that he might be in deadly danger seemed ludicrous — but half an hour ago, the idea that he was adopted would have seemed just as unlikely. He slid out of bed and went looking in the closet for his clothes. There was no sign of them.

He winced as he realized that they must have been covered in his blood. They would have had to have been destroyed. He'd have to get some new ones.

The door opened and Dr. Morton strode in. The smile was gone from her face. "What do you think you're doing? Get back into bed this moment." Mora came in behind her, looking worried.

"Sorry, Doctor," Tristan answered. "I've got to get moving. Something urgent has come up. Now, I need to get some clothes."

"You're not leaving here until I say you're well enough to go," Dr. Morton said stubbornly. "And I want you in for observation for another day."

"Come and visit me if you want to observe me," Tristan replied. "You can't keep me here against my will. And you wouldn't be able to keep me here without posting guards on the door. I don't think you're quite prepared to do that — are you?"

The doctor hesitated, but Tristan sensed that he'd won. It would be unlawful imprisonment if she kept him here once he'd stated his desire to leave, and the hospital could be InstaSued. If it was, she'd lose her job. "This is very unadvisable," she finally said.

"Yeah, I'm the headstrong type," Tristan agreed. "Now, about some clothes . . . ?"

"I'll arrange it," Dr. Morton agreed, caving in. "But I want you to be careful. I'm sure you've got a Housebot that can monitor your readings. I want you to do that twice a day, and have it transmit me the results. Promise me that."

"Okay." Tristan would have promised her anything in order to get out.

"Here." She gave him a card with her Terminal number. Then, after one last, irritated look, she marched out of the room.

"You're quite forceful when you want to be," Mora said, grinning. "I think I like this new you."

"It's desperation," Tristan confessed. "I'm starting to feel trapped. I'm sure it's just my imagination, but I'm starting to feel that things are closing in on me." He stared at the door. "Come on, come *on*!"

Shimoda stood in her small office in the Computer Control building and breathed a prayer of thanks that it was still hers. She had been fortunate. The board wasn't noted for accepting failure. Still, she *hadn't* failed yet, and she wasn't going to. "Terminal," she called. "Check monitoring systems."

"All functional," her Terminal replied.

"Special scan for *Quietus*?"

"That program has priority status," the Terminal assured her.

"Good." Shimoda walked to the window and looked out on the Garden of Peace in Tokyo. It wasn't actually there, of course, since the "window" was merely a Screen. But it did her soul good to gaze out at the beauty of the garden. It reminded her of her heritage, even though she and the previous three generations of her family had been born in what had once been the United States. Blood was stronger than soil when it came to heritage.

Everything was ready. She knew that her program worms would catch anything like the killer virus if it got loose again, and would alert her to anything on the Net dealing with Quietus. Until something happened, there wasn't much else she could do.

The big question, of course, was: Would anything happen? Or had whoever set that virus going finished with whatever they had been planning? If it had been a random act of senseless violence, then none of her worms would do any good. The person responsible for all of those deaths would go uncaught. But Shimoda had been in police work all her adult life, and every instinct told her that the person who had done this was just getting started.

Of course, that meant that next time the killer struck, it was bound to be on a bigger scale, with far worse effects. She could only pray that she would be able to track and stop the villain in time.

Staring out of the window, she focused on the garden and strove to clear her mind of all worries and fears. She had to be ready when the next attack came.

Genia had enjoyed her day. Thanks to Mr. Rikard Lytton she'd had a wonderful meal yesterday and had been able to return home with some much-needed stores. She had food now to last her a week, and some nice new clothes, too. She examined the clingy silver jumpsuit and knee-high black boots in her mirror. She looked good, no question about it. And the sleeves of the costume, as always, were loose enough to hide her scanner. She didn't need to go hunting again for quite a while.

She looked around her room and felt some satisfaction. She'd taken over an abandoned third-floor suite in an old hotel. First floor would have been asking for trouble, and even third floor would have been pushing it if she hadn't installed her own security equipment. (Trespassers would be fried. . . .) The rooms had been dingy and depressing when she'd found them a year ago, like the rest of the Underworld tended to be. They'd been abandoned for over fifty years, after all. But Genia had seen the potential in the rooms, and had decided they would do.

In that year, she'd redecorated them totally, and had her own Cleaningbot that fussed to keep them beautiful. One room was for the Terminal and her workshop, which the 'bot was forbidden to enter. She didn't want her latest work to be considered junk and cleaned up, after all. Another room was her living room and bedroom. She'd never managed to get used to sleeping in beds, like those folk Above tended to do. Instead, she had a mass of pillows and cushions in the corner of the room, with a comforter thrown over them. She had a large Screen (with stolen, untraceable satellite access), and a holoprojector. She could make her rooms look like anything she chose. Strangely, perhaps, she preferred them to show what was really there.

There was a large window, looking out on the Underworld and the floor of Above, just two stories over her head. She liked to look at the floor because it reminded her that she wasn't considered to be a real person. Just some statistic in forgotten reports. Nobody cared who or how many lived in the Underworld. Most people Above didn't even know that there was such a place, and certainly never spared a thought for the poor people who lived there. Genia understood the system by which Above lived, and could prey on them. She wasn't just nameless, forgotten Underworld trash; she was Genia. "The feminine of *genius*," she liked to say with a grin. And she believed it.

She wasn't a part of either world, and she despised them both. All they were good for was to let her live exactly as she wanted.

But *what* did she want? What was she going to do with herself? With her state-of-the-art Terminal, she could travel anywhere she wished. At her fingertips were the frozen wastes of Antarctica or the frigid wastes of the lunar seas. She could chase comets out in the reaches of the solar system (they had just finished scanning in Pluto), or dive into sacred wells in Mexico to hunt the treasures of the Aztecs. All worlds were open to her. Or she could download the latest entertainment directly to her Screen. But, to be honest, none of this appealed to her. She could work on her new scanner. It was always good to have a backup, just in case, and she'd come up with a few nice little improvements. But today didn't feel like a workday.

"I want to shop," she decided. It had been fun yesterday picking out new clothes. Today, she realized, she wanted to have some fun. "Toys," she murmured. Something to play with, to distract her.

And that meant going Above again. Nobody would deliver to an address in the Underworld, not even the dumbest Deliverybot. Genia liked the idea of walking up there again. She enjoyed passing herself off as one of the elite, knowing she was far, far better than them. And there were always victims to be found and exploited.

Her mind made up, Genia moved to the door. "Terminal," she called out. "Set all security measures in fifteen seconds." She left her rooms and closed the doors. As she was walking away, the security protocols came on-line, making her apartment into a miniature fortress. No casual thief would be able to get in there — nor would a more sophisticated one. She'd written unhackable programs, and the defenses were designed to kill, not maim. She might be able to rob with impunity, but nobody took anything from her.

Nobody.

5

Devon simply didn't understand people. The more he watched them, the less he could figure them out. But it was an addiction, and he couldn't bring himself to stop. He had his Screen on almost twenty-four hours a day. He could sleep through the low murmur — in fact, he couldn't sleep if it was turned off. The only times he ever muted it were when he had visitors.

He almost never had visitors.

Devon liked it like that. He knew what people were like; he'd been watching them all his life. Using home security monitors he could flick back and forth, watching homes, without their occupants being aware of his interest. He saw how untidy people were, and this irritated him. In his world, everything was in place, precisely where it was supposed to be. With his eyes closed, he could reach for anything he needed and *know* that it was there. The idea of other people touching anything that belonged to him made him shudder.

No, his world was *his*, and his alone. He could never share space with another human being. So he had never managed to understand why anyone else did.

He flicked on one monitor, and his Terminal brought up the picture for him to observe. He didn't know who it was, or even where in the world. It didn't make much difference, of course; they were just people, and there were billions of them, all unimportant in the grand scheme of things.

Unlike Devon, who was very, very important. These people were nothings. But, somehow, they intrigued him.

The monitors in this house were set up in most rooms. Not the bathroom, of course — nobody wanted *that* to be monitored! — but every other room, including the children's bedrooms. And Devon could watch any time he wished. It was breakfast time where the family lived, which suggested they were about six hours behind Devon's time, since he had recently eaten his lunch. Not that this mattered. He didn't care where they were, really. But breakfast time was always particularly revolting. The family consisted of two parents and four children. That was large, really, but even if it wasn't typical, it gave Devon more to study. The parents were both in their forties, with dull jobs. The oldest girl was sixteen, the oldest boy twelve. Then there were twins, a boy and girl, both six. It was the twins who had drawn Devon to this family to begin with. He'd been intrigued with the thought of two human beings, so alike and yet so different. Both had short-cropped blond hair, and they did have a lot in common. But the girl was messy and the boy a neatness freak — a boy after Devon's own heart.

Breakfast was like feeding time at the zoo. They all wanted something different, and generally they all wanted their choices at the same time as everyone else. The Kitchenbot had to prioritize, which always caused arguments. Devon watched with distaste as the older girl and the younger verbally sparred over who should have the first helping of hot cereal when it had been zapped up.

Families! Yuck!

The boys resented having the girls go first, but the

parents were adamant that this was the correct order, and the kids had stopped arguing about that, at least. Devon couldn't see the logic in this decision, but he'd discovered long ago that "logic" had very little to do with the behavior of this family.

Eventually they were all eating, and Devon got bored. They'd be going to their rooms and logging in to school next. They were pathetically slow, the older girl still in thirteenth grade. Devon had passed through that a decade earlier. He felt a faint contempt for her lack of mental ability. It was probably her upbringing, he knew, and it was unfair to despise her because of that. The other three were even slower than she was.

Well, he'd come back when they had more interactions with other people. That wouldn't be for hours yet, of course. Devon shrugged, and began to search for something to occupy himself. Some more news footage of his recent actions would be fun, but he didn't think there would be much. It was already over a day old, and news died fast.

"— their list of the top one hundred films of the twenty-first century," one of the anchors was saying. He adjusted his bright silver tie, smiling insincerely. "To nobody's surprise, the top director was Leonardo DiCaprio. Three of his movies made the list, with his much-loved masterpiece, *I, Clinton*, taking top honors. The film, about the presidency and decline of the aging statesman, has garnered numerous awards since its initial release in 2032. Naturally, no movie released in the last six months made the list. The most recent was Sylvester Stallone V's *Martian Heat*, one of his most popular action flicks. In other news —"

Devon sighed and turned away. Over a hundred years ago, Andy Warhol had said that everyone would have fifteen minutes of fame. It looked as though his fifteen minutes were over.

For now.

But, of course, he had only just begun. Very soon, the Doomsday Virus would be finished, and then the fun would *really* start.

Tristan sat in his bedroom, hesitating. He was alone now, since his parents believed that Dr. Morton had released him. Tristan hadn't exactly lied to them, but he'd allowed them to believe this. They had both returned to their own rooms to get back to work. Mora had reluctantly gone home, with a promise to come back the next day. Tristan could tell that she didn't think he was really in any danger, but that she was worried for him anyway. Now that Tristan was alone, he was slightly reluctant to begin the search that he knew he must undertake. The only place he would be able to find out his real identity was in the .comworld. He was fourteen, born in 2085. And everyone had been giving DNA samples for access to the Net for almost twenty years. So his birth parents would be there, even if they had died after he was born.

The question was, did he *really* want to know who he was? He wasn't sure. For one thing, Mom and Dad still felt like real parents to him. They had, after all, raised him from the day of his birth, and he knew without a doubt that they both loved him. Would it be fair to them to go hunting for other parents? On the other hand, could he live without knowing the truth?

Then there was the matter of Dr. Taru's warning. If he discovered the truth about himself, would he accidentally alert somebody that he was still alive? Would they come after him, after all these years?

He didn't know. He was pretty sure he could cover his tracks so that nobody could trace him. And surely it had to be worth running a risk in order to know the truth?

He made up his mind to do it. His Terminal was pretty sophisticated, linked through his father's bank, First Security International. Dad was a vice president, and quite highly placed, so he rated a Level Five Terminal.

Along with voice and holoprojection features, it had a speedboard, on which Tristan preferred to work. Voice command was fine, but it took forever to speak coding. For some things, nothing beat a speedboard.

He typed the commands, running his guard dog worms out into the Net. They'd hover there, watching for any incoming messages or worms. If they found any, they'd stomp them to death, giving him time to cut the link before he could be traced.

Once the guard dogs were up and running protection, Tristan reverted to voice command.

"Terminal, check my DNA records," he ordered.

"DNA records on file," the Terminal replied.

"Good. Now access the DNA data banks."

"Restricted and protected information," the Terminal said promptly and a little smugly. Naturally, neither Tristan nor anyone outside of Computer Control was supposed to get into such files. They were theoretically hackerproof.

But theories are often wrong.

"Call up the protection," he ordered, returning to his speedboard and monitor. The access information scrolled up. *Encrypted, password triple-guarded, watchworms . . .* It was heavily protected indeed. But not heavily enough, if he had sufficient motivation. This was where he'd find his parents, and nobody was going to keep him out.

What he was doing was, of course, highly illegal. This didn't really bother Tristan. He wasn't doing this for any criminal reason. He just wanted to know the identities of his birth parents.

He started by selectively disabling the watch-worms. They were programmed to neutralize anyone who tried to break in. But he wasn't breaking in — yet! — so they just hovered there. He couldn't disable them entirely. If he did, Computer Control was bound to notice. And, besides that, it would mean anyone else could break in like this, and anyone else who tried was bound to be a criminal. He didn't want to leave them an open invitation to pillage at will.

So instead, he hid his access. The watch-worms would patrol as normal, only when they came to his small area they would be selectively blind. Once he cut the connection, they'd be able to see perfectly well again, so no lasting damage would be done.

It took Tristan almost half an hour of work before he was certain that the worms could no longer detect him. Then it was time for the triple-guards. The three separate systems had to be decoded and entered, and the correct passwords had to be given within a ten-second time frame. This was nasty, but not impossible. He had a prime number search engine he'd written a year or so before that crunched numbers like a dog crunches bones. He set it working on the first of the guards, and while it hunted he checked for other safeguards. There was bound to be at least one hidden, and more likely two or three. Computer Control wasn't complacent.

The search engine whistled once, showing it had the first command override. He ignored it, hunting for the traps. It whistled for the second before he found what he was looking for. A sneaky little gateway trap. Once the three commands were entered, there would be a brief pause, during which he'd have to supply a fourth password. Otherwise, the system would lock him out. Tristan was sure he could beat it. The engine whistled for the third and last time; he had the basic information. Now he needed the password. There was only an eight-second margin, so it couldn't be anything elaborate. He hunted, and checked, and then grinned when he found it. A single word! *Good-bye.* Not what you'd normally type when you entered a system.

He switched back to the search engine, calling up the three passwords. Taking a deep breath, he tapped ENTER. A second later, he typed GOOD-BYE.

"Access granted," his Terminal murmured. He was

certain it was just his imagination, but the Terminal even sounded slightly impressed. After all, he'd broken into one of the most secure files in the world, and now all the information he needed was at his fingertips.

He had power that only Computer Control was supposed to have. He had *everything* available to him.

But he only wanted one thing.

"Terminal," he ordered, "scan the files for the closest DNA match to my own. I want you to pull up any records that are close enough to my own to be distant relatives. Up to five relationships away." *Relationships* — was that the right word? He didn't know. But he wanted to identify potential uncles and aunts and cousins as well. He didn't want to exclude anyone just yet.

He waited impatiently as the computer scanned the files. There were six billion-plus entries in here, each with a complex biological code. It would take some time for his unit to scan those. He took a sip of soda as he waited. He was on edge. Not just because he might get caught — and if he was caught, he'd definitely go to jail, no matter why he'd done what he had. But also because he was on the verge of finding out his true identity.

"Finished," the Terminal announced. "No matches have been found."

"What?" Shock and disappointment swamped his mind. "That's impossible! There has to be somebody in there who is related to me!"

"No matching records have been found under assigned parameters," the Terminal insisted. "There are no relationships registered closer than twelve moves."

Twelve moves? What was that? It had to be very, very distant cousins or something. "How many of those?" he asked.

"Approximately twenty thousand," the Terminal replied. "Statistically, they cannot be close relatives."

Nobody! Tristan cried wordlessly, venting his anger, disappointment, and frustration. What the computer was telling him was absolutely impossible. It was saying that he had no father or mother, no siblings — not even uncles or grandparents. And that simply couldn't be the case.

What was wrong?

6

Tristan sat thinking furiously for a couple of minutes. There were only two possible reasons for his failure to find anything: Either there was nothing to find, or else the information had been removed.

However, only a few people in the .comworld could have made Tristan's files disappear. He knew for himself how difficult breaking in was. And then to erase something and leave no trace? It would take a greater hacker than even he was. And Tristan knew most of the hackers, at least by name. Nobody he knew had this ability. Maybe a Control official would have the power, but why would one of them alter the records?

Could it be somebody that Tristan had never suspected? Perhaps his birth parents?

Or the people who might be after him?

There was nothing more he could do here, but he couldn't simply leave. He didn't want to leave the DNA files without creating a way back in, just in case he should need it. The information he needed might be here, and it would be foolish to try breaking in again. Instead, he began to fabricate a fake "authorized" account for himself. This wasn't easy, but it was a lot simpler than breaking in unnoticed a second or third time. He had to make sure the account was hidden from any routine virus scans. He didn't want it being detected and traced to him. Then, finally, he used the scanner to verify his DNA code as the only one to access the account.

"Confirmed," the Terminal replied. "This is now your third account."

What?

Tristan's head jerked up. "Terminal," he said slowly. "Confirm that information. This is my *third* account?"

"Correct."

"List the accounts in order of establishment dates,

starting with today's," he ordered. What was going on here?

"2099," the computer said. "Account for Centrus." That was the on-line name he'd given himself for his "authorized" entry. "It is now being hidden and will not register again on any search. 2083. Account for Tristan Connor. 2082. Account for Quietus."

"Huh?" Tristan was totally lost here. Not only had he never used the name *Quietus*, but it had been registered a year before he was born! And it had been the name Dr. Taru had warned his parents against. This didn't sound good.

Why would his supposed foe have an account matching only Tristan's DNA?

He took a deep breath. Maybe his parents had done this? After all, it was possible that a DNA sample had been taken from him while he was a fetus, and an account set up then. Weird, but possible. This could be very dangerous, but there was obviously only one thing to do.

"Terminal," he commanded. "Access account Quietus."

Shimoda jerked back to full alertness in a fraction of a second when her Terminal started flashing lights at her.

"What is it?" she demanded. All thoughts of the peaceful garden were now well out of her mind.

"Someone has accessed the Net using the name *Quietus*," her Terminal informed her. "Scanning for location."

Shimoda thought fast. "It's not one of the board members searching for information, is it?" she asked. She didn't want to get her hopes up unduly.

"Negative," the Terminal replied. "Access, however, is from within Control itself."

"What?" Shimoda was startled. The accounts here were the most secure in the world. "Explain."

"Unable to explain," the computer answered. "Tracing the intruder."

Shimoda stared at the blank wall, excitement rising. This was what she had been waiting for! Her saboteur was trying to strike again. And this time Shimoda would catch the criminal.

Tristan was puzzled but excited as he bent to his task. As he had commanded, the computer had accessed the Quietus account and projected the result in the air in front of him. It turned out to be a sequence of codes, obviously protection against someone breaking in to the account. He didn't know how long it would keep him out, but it wouldn't be forever.

As he worked, he tried to make sense of what he'd found. He didn't have any clue yet as to what was in these files, except that they took up a lot of memory. They were big, then, and well protected. Was this the secret of his past?

One by one, Tristan worked his way through the safeguards that surrounded access to the account. They were tricky, and one or two were fierce, but they were all well within his ability to handle.

It was tough work, but Tristan was thorough and logical. Each barrier eventually crumbled before him; he typed in the final password, and he had access.

To what?

There was only one file here, and it was labeled DOOMSDAY.

He stared at the name that wavered slightly in the air before his face. *Doomsday?* What could that mean?

The only way to know was to run it. If this was something his parents had left for him, he had to know what was in it. The name disturbed him, however, and he hesitated. It might simply be a trap set to see if he ever showed up.

Tristan didn't know what to do. Trap or information? He stood up and paced his room, trying to make up his mind. He had the safeguards in place, after all. If anyone tried to trap him, he should be able to break out without being traced. On the other hand, this account was specifically triggered by his DNA. If the triggering showed up anywhere, whoever had set the program would know that he was alive. He might already be in danger.

Right on cue, there was barking from the computer. His guard dogs were warning him that somebody was on his trail. They would fight off any such attempt, but they couldn't battle forever. He would have to quit this place very soon.

His mind was made up. If someone was after him, he or she might already know he existed. He had nothing to lose now.

"Terminal," he ordered, "run program Doomsday."

Genia was in a good mood. She sat in the booth in the First Security International Bank, finishing her transfers. Ms. Betti Cartmel had kindly donated several thousand credits — though she wouldn't be aware of the fact for a few days — and Genia's purchases were already arriving at the hotel room she'd booked. Now all she had to do was to wipe out all records from the Terminal and backtrack the cameras. But this time it wasn't so easy.

Genia froze, staring at the screen in disbelief.

Something was going very, very wrong with the bank's computers. Instead of the usual friendly pictures of money being transferred, suddenly the little green slips of what had once been called bank notes were igniting and burning. And the little picture of the bank had started to crumble apart.

And over this, in bloodred letters, appeared the words DIE, SUCKERS!!!

"Program running," the Terminal confirmed.

Tristan watched as an image of the world was called up on the projector, hovering almost close enough to touch. A small dot marked his home in New York, and then a stream of light from above the globe flashed down to touch the spark.

"Doomsday Virus initiated and downloading," the Terminal announced.

Virus?

Tristan stared at the picture in horror. A Doomsday

virus? That could only mean one thing . . . a program that was self-replicating, and that was meant to destroy all other programs it encountered.

It would devour everything in its path. It would spread throughout the Net, erasing *everything* — programs, information, codes . . .

The end of the Net. And, without the Net, the end of the world itself. *Everything* these days depended on the Net. Everything . . .

And he had just unleashed a lethal virus into it . . .

7

What have I done?

Tristan felt sick and scared; the killer virus would ravage everywhere and destroy everything. . . .

Unless he could somehow stop it.

Images flashed through his head. *Elevators falling, carrying helpless, screaming people to their deaths many floors below — because the computer controls had been destroyed. Factories exploding, maiming and killing workers. Aircraft plunging from the skies, their navcoms fried . . .*

Feverishly, he started working. He didn't know how

long he had, but it was most likely a matter of a couple of minutes, tops. He *had* to kill the virus by then. He didn't know if he had the skills, but he did know he had to try, before the whole world crashed around him.

.comlibraries wiped, all information being destroyed. Records — police, bank, personal — vanished, never to be retrieved. Screens dying. People staring in horror, with no access to news, information, communications, anything . . .

The first thing he did was to call in his guard dogs. They were meant to devour any program, and if he could redirect them after Doomsday they would at least be able to slow it down, if not stop it completely. Of course, they were his only protection now against discovery, and they had warned him that somebody was trying to trace him already. Setting them onto Doomsday would leave him exposed. But to be honest, that was almost the least of his fears right now. He had to prevent the world from collapsing. . . .

Buildings in flames because the fire department couldn't move and didn't know there was a problem. People dying, unable to get help from a hospital. People in the hospitals dying because their bedcoms couldn't monitor their conditions . . .

The dogs whirled around and shot after Doomsday, as he ordered. Then, ignoring the panic that was icing up his spine, Tristan set to work building a barrier behind them that would contain even the killer virus.

And all of it his fault!

If he only had the time . . .

Shimoda could feel a surge of excitement, knowing that she was closing in on her villain. The fiend was smart enough to leave traps, of course, but she'd been expecting that. At her Terminal she was working as fast as she could, trying to break past the attack programs guarding the culprit's trail. She hated to admit it, but they were ferociously capable and she wasn't absolutely sure that she could manage it. Sweat started to trickle down her brow as she worked, but she ignored it.

There was something odd about this. Shimoda had laid in a second command, once the Quietus code had been sounded, to track anything being fed to the Newsbots. The crook was publicity-hungry, and he was bound to alert the media so they could cover his next planned disaster. Only, according to her computer nobody had hacked into the Newsbots this time. Why wouldn't the perp alert the news again?

Maybe because he didn't want this attack to be spotted? What if the first three were simply to make her *think* he wanted publicity? So that when he did what he *really* wanted, she might ignore it, thinking it was a false alarm? Shimoda grinned to herself. It made sense. But she was too smart to be fooled by that trick!

Then, suddenly, the attack programs were gone. She blinked, amazed and then afraid that she'd been detected and the culprit had fled. Then she saw that the link through Control was still there. The programs had been called off for some reason. . . .

It didn't make any sense, but she couldn't afford to be slow or too suspicious here. Maybe it was a trap. Maybe the perp *wanted* her to follow. It didn't matter. If she didn't take this chance, she'd lose the link and wouldn't be able to stop this maniac. She *had* to assume that her foe was facing a genuine problem and would act accordingly.

She started after the fleeing programs, tracking them back to their master or mistress. She would have her criminal this time. . . .

Genia stared at the monitor in shock. There was a visual ripping through the Screen now — a bloated purple dragon, tearing little buildings to pieces and eating screaming figures. The "creature" was all teeth and claws, and there was a loud, technopunk sound track blaring as it attacked its tiny victims. Somebody had to be downloading a computer virus into the bank's files. A thrill ran through her as she realized what this had to mean. It was a bank robbery in progress! Somebody must have looted the bank's records, and was now destroying all evidence of their tampering. It was a really crude solution, nowhere near as elegant as her own method, but it could well work simply because it was brutally efficient. If the computers were wiped, then nothing could be traced by anyone.

She was about to disengage herself when she had another thought.

The virus would destroy the bank's information, but she was a lot smarter than the bank. And the virus command code might well tell her who had written it. If she could isolate a fragment — and no more, or her own systems might be wiped! — then it would be like having a signed confession from the crook. She could get a lot of money from whoever was behind this not to turn the evidence over to the police. . . .

Genia's fingers were flying as she typed in command codes. It was going to be a very delicate job, but she knew she was fast and clever enough to pull it off. All she needed was a quick program to snip a piece of the virus's central coding. And her scanner device already had something like that, so she could just adapt it! Grinning happily, Genia set about sampling the virus code.

The dragon was growing, second by second, as it devoured more and more of its simulated victims. The music roared even louder than the dragon as it ravaged the bank's files, destroying everything as it fed.

How long before it copied itself and began to spread?

Sweat was pouring down Tristan's face and back as he worked as swiftly as he could to isolate and kill the virus. In the back of his mind he knew that there was somebody tracking him, but he had to ignore that problem. Stopping the virus dead was the most important thing right now.

Even as he worked, he could see that the Doomsday Virus was ravaging the bank's mainframe. It had manifested itself as a mythological dragon, wreaking havoc as it stomped a town flat. The form wasn't real, of course, but had been selected by the virus's creator as a representation. And it was quite a terrifying one as it flattened everything it came across, absorbing the wreckage and growing. He could see the panic that it was setting off as all the bank's computers crashed, one after another. Information was being devoured, leaving no traces. People would be unable to access their accounts, pay bills, or even use the phones.

And, as it attacked, the virus bred. The dragon was laying eggs, which then cracked open. Tiny dragons broke free and started to engulf whatever was close to them. All colors of the spectrum, these tiny destroyers worked their way through the system, swallowing up more information and breeding again. In a matter of a minute or less, the virus would reach the edge of the bank's portion of the Net, and would then be able to download itself directly into the Net. Once it was there, nothing could stop its feeding frenzy. It would engulf all information it came across, ripping it to pieces and rebuilding it in its own image. It would cause a domino effect, shattering everything, one step at a time.

Soon there would be nothing left but hungry dragons, snatching up and eating whatever they came across. Once they were in the Net, they would be unstoppable.

He had to prevent their escape.

The guard dogs closed in, guarding the exits from the

mainframe and tearing into the virus as it moved. His Doberman facsimiles ripped the dragons apart, devouring the virus instead of being destroyed. But there were so many dragons, and so few dogs. Tristan prayed they could hold the virus off long enough. What he had to do was to isolate the bank totally, knocking out its connection to the Net. That was, of course, theoretically impossible. The bank's computer programmers would have safeguards to stop anyone from doing that.

But he was better than any bank programmer. The weak link here was the telephone connection. Without that, the bank would be isolated. The dragons had already almost obliterated its records, but they were still contained. If he could cut the connection, they could howl around the bank computer all they liked. Tristan attacked the program that kept the bank hooked to the Net, ripping through its weak defenses. The bank security programs fought back, but they were no match for his skill. One by one, he shut down the safeguards, and his final guard dog figuratively ripped free the connection.

The link with the Net was severed. His Screen died.

But had he been in time? His own computer was connected through his father's bank. Whatever happened, that mainframe was dead, ravaged by the virus. He wouldn't be able to log back on again. But his hand-comp was through a separate but limited server. He quickly uplinked it and logged in.

He breathed a sigh of relief as he reached the Net. A quick scan showed that nothing had been affected. Then he tried to tap back into his bank account. "System unavailable," his hand-comp responded.

So he'd managed to isolate First Security International from the rest of the Web in time! He'd stopped the virus from destroying everything. All that was gone were the bank records.

All!

That meant *his* money, for one thing, and the family's. It meant thousands if not millions of customers cut off. It meant a mountain of trouble. But it was still better than it could have been.

He couldn't tell anyone what he had done. If the police found out, he'd be jailed for life. His hands were shaking as he disconnected from the Net and collapsed backward in his chair.

He was a criminal! He hadn't meant to unleash that virus. He hadn't even known of its existence. But that would hardly be a great defense to use. He *had* deliberately hacked into Computer Central, after all. And he had set the virus free.

Tristan felt as if he'd betrayed everything he'd ever believed in. In fact, even if not in his heart, he was a criminal. An unwitting one, but that hardly excused his horrible behavior. He had almost destroyed the Net through his own incredible stupidity. He was going to be in a huge amount of trouble if anyone found out that he was involved in any way. He didn't know what to do yet, but he knew what he couldn't do — he couldn't tell anyone anything at all about it. Even his parents would be forced to report him if they found out. He'd just have to play ignorant and pretend that he was as surprised and appalled as anyone over what had happened.

He started shaking again. There was that person who'd been trying to trace him! Had he been discovered? If the hacker had managed to find him before he had cut the bank free, then he or she would have his address.

His stomach wanted to kill him. Groaning, he lurched to the bathroom and took a shot of antinausea. His nerves were eating at him and he waited, agonizing in his mind, to see if he was going to be arrested. The worse thing was that he knew he deserved it.

What could he ever do to make amends?

Shimoda almost screamed in frustration as her probe abruptly terminated. She slammed her fist down beside her Terminal and yelped at the resulting pain.

"Contact has been lost," her Terminal said gravely.

"Reconnect with the First Security International Bank," she ordered.

"Unable to comply. The bank Terminals are down."

"Down?"

"The virus has destroyed all records."

Shimoda stared into the air, shocked. Now she *knew* what had happened, without a doubt. Her criminal had ransacked the accounts at the bank, transferring out who knew how much money, and had then used the virus to destroy the bank's computers to prevent the losses being traced. Overkill, to be sure, but effective.

And she had *lost* the crook!

She could feel a migraine headache starting up. This failure could cost her her job. Unless . . . "I need a list of all the bank's customers," she said quickly, hoping this would work.

"The list is unavailable," the Terminal answered. "All records have been lost."

Typical Terminal thinking! "People will be calling in to complain that their accounts are inaccessible," she said carefully. "Monitor the calls, and list all who do so." She was gambling here a bit, she knew. What if the crook didn't complain that his or her funds were missing? Then Shimoda would be out of luck. But she was willing to bet that the crook would try to cover all tracks by acting like he or she had lost money, too.

It was a long shot.

But it was the only shot she had.

8

enia had fled the immediate vicinity of the bank as soon as she could. All thoughts of going on a shopping spree vanished from her mind. The only thing she could think about was the computer virus that had destroyed the bank records.

She wasn't the only one obsessing on that, of course. Newsbots were gathering over the city, she could see. Genia hurried to the public Screen in Times Square and watched the latest information. It was horrendous.

Even the news anchor looked shocked for once. They were mostly smooth Hollywood types who didn't emote even during the worst of news. Not that there was a lot of bad news these days. But this well-groomed man looked close to tears as he informed the public that First Security International had completely collapsed. All records were gone, including even basics such as the names of people who had deposits with them. There was now no record of their financial lives.

People were starting to panic. Without bank accounts, they couldn't buy anything or get medical help. Even their .comNet was down, and they couldn't call anyone to complain. Not that anything could be done, because there were simply no remaining records. Terminal printouts, of course, had been banned in 2078 because they wasted paper. The thought then was that a bank crash was absolutely impossible.

But the impossible had happened.

There were backups, of course. The bank kept the same information in six different locations, in case one of their mainframes should break down. The thought that all six might break down was inconceivable. But all six had been wiped.

As Genia watched the Screen, she saw the swooping shots of Newsbots as they converged on City Hall. (It wasn't as if there was a bank building to descend upon — the whole operation existed on the Net.) Her

eyes widened as she saw a small crowd of people —
perhaps thirty strong — moving grimly toward the
pseudomarble building. It was almost a riot! Genia
glanced around. Times Square was a tourist spot so it
was rather crowded. There were five other people here
with her. Thirty marching on City Hall spelled trouble,
that was for sure.

Well, she couldn't blame them. How many people's
lives had just been ruined by the virus? How many
people would soon be without heat, shelter, food, or
medical supplies? As soon as their bank accounts dis-
solved, some people's utilities would be shut off. And
what could anyone do about it? She was certain that
there were no emergency plans for such a situation.

But she couldn't feel too sorry for those people.
They'd lived the good life until now, unlike her and the
others in the Underworld. "Welcome to reality," she
muttered, watching the panicking people with a certain measure of satisfaction. "Learn to live with it. *I*
have to."

But she knew in her heart that they wouldn't be able
to do this. They were naive, too used to having their
whims catered to, their orders followed, and their lives
ordered for them. This was going to be major trouble.
And those thirty people were literally just the tip of the

iceberg. There had to be many thousands, if not more, scattered around the whole world, in the same situation, only without the ability to march to complain.

It was going to get worse — much worse — as the day wore on.

She stared in awe at the small chip she held. She'd managed to get a little of the computer virus onto the chip. It was programmed to wipe out everything, but she was able to build a buffer in time to contain it. It wouldn't hold the complete virus, of course, but she'd made a quick hack-and-slash raid, taking only a chunk of the program. It wasn't enough for the virus to reproduce itself and feed, but it was enough for her to try to isolate and identify it.

There couldn't be more than about a dozen people in the world capable of writing a program like this. It was way too sophisticated for the average hacker. Even she couldn't have managed this without a lot of time and effort.

All code writers had their own particular ways of doing things. If she could isolate some bands of the code and then cross-check them with legitimate samples from the various suspects, she was pretty sure she could identify the creator of the virus.

And then? Obviously whoever had created it had used

it to rob one of the richest banks in the world. They should be willing to pay big bucks not to be turned over to the police. And if they weren't, the police were likely to pay quite well for information leading to an arrest. With a grin, Genia patted the little chip. This could be her key out of the Underworld and into the Above. . . .

Or, if she messed this up, it could be her key out of the Underworld and into a very early grave . . .

Devon was alternating between fury and panic as he stared at the readouts. How *could* this have happened? Somehow, the Doomsday Virus had been accessed and released. He had halted it as soon as his Terminal had informed him of the problem. But it had been too late. The virus had downloaded into the mainframe of some bank or another, and run amuck.

And then, strangely, it had stopped.

That was almost as scary as its inexplicable release. Doomsday was written to be unstoppable.

How had it been stopped?

Devon cursed as he stomped around his room, and then managed to focus his mind. "Terminal," he snarled, "how was Doomsday unleashed? Isn't it coded to my command only?"

"Yes," the Terminal replied calmly. "Checking. You gave the command."

"I did *not* give the command!" Devon yelled. "Check again!"

There was the barest of pauses. "The records indicate that you did indeed give the command."

"Impossible." Devon couldn't understand it.

"The command was given and verified," the Terminal continued. "Your account was accessed using your DNA, and then Doomsday was triggered."

That didn't make any sense at all. Unless, somehow, somebody had managed to get a sample of his DNA without his knowledge. He stayed in his suite of rooms at all times. He never allowed his rare visitors to get close to him, let alone touch him. All his hair cuttings, toenail clippings, *anything* was instantly destroyed. There was no way for anyone to get his DNA samples.

Well, *almost* no way. Rumor had it that in the Underworld many things were possible that theoretically couldn't exist. The government thought it had managed to control crime by using the ICs, but they were living in a fool's paradise. Hypothetically, the system worked perfectly. Everyone had an IC put in their wrist at birth. And these chips were read by machines constantly. The government could flawlessly trace the movements of anyone with an IC. Wherever you walked, whatever you did, you left a trail. This meant that most conventional crimes were impossible. Murder? The government could place you at the scene of the killing at the exact time it occurred. Robbery? Muggings? The same — the government knew where you were at all times. No possible alibis, no excuses. You'd be nailed.

And Control thought *that* would eliminate crime! It just went to show how stupid and complacent they were. Crime wasn't eliminated, it simply changed, as it always had. Devon loved to read about the history of crime. One of his heroes was Jesse James, who had figured out the weakness of what was then a new technology — the railroad — and evolved a method of robbing it. *That* was how crime continued — abandoning the old methods and inventing new ones.

Undoubtedly, there were people in the Underworld who could do things with computers that were supposed to be impossible. If anyone could hack into his account, it had to be one of them. Whoever it was would think that he or she was untraceable, of course. And, normally, they would be right.

But Devon wasn't normal, and if he managed to get on the person's trail he'd never be shaken free.

He grabbed his speedboard and started working. The

records of the bank had been wiped out by the virus, of course, so he couldn't get to the information he needed that way. But there was more than one way to skin a cat. A stupid expression, really, because nobody ever had a use for a catskin, but it was accurate. He couldn't access the bank records, but he *could* access the line records.

Whoever had logged in to the bank and broken into his account had to have been on the line at the time to do it. So all he needed to do was to find out who had done that. It took all of two minutes to find the list of names. It would have been faster if he hadn't been forced to override the security protocols at the line database. These records showed that there had been eighty-four people on the bank lines at the time of the virus's release. Fine. Now, if he was lucky, he would be able to eliminate all but one of those names.

If a hacker had stolen an identity to break into the bank, there was a good possibility that the identity stolen belonged to someone who was also on-line at the time, somewhere else. . . .

"Check these names against other database records," he informed the Terminal. "See if any of them were on-line elsewhere at the same time."

"One," the Terminal answered within seconds. "Betti Cartmel."

Devon grinned. He'd lucked out — the thief *was* there! "Bring up the records," he ordered. The Screen split to show both log-ons. One was from a home in the city, the other from a bank Terminal. Since the Terminal belonged to First Security International, this was obviously the most likely choice. The problem was he couldn't access the bank's security records, since they'd been wiped along with everything else. If he only knew what the thief looked like, it would be a help.

Quickly he called up a map of the city, narrowing in on the plaza where the bank was located. Then he looked around for other security cameras in the area. He knew the time he was looking for, barely ten minutes ago now . . . and there was one. Winston Securities had a front-door surveillance camera, and its field overlooked the bank's access booths.

He called up the record. While he was accessing it, he checked on the location of Betti Cartmel. There was now only one IC trace, showing her at the home his Terminal had located. The second one had vanished. There were no IC records of her ever entering or leaving the bank. So it *was* a hacker, who had kept the chip dormant until he or she had entered the bank's access booth, and then switched it off immediately afterward.

The on-line recording was ready, and Devon played it eagerly. The access booth he was interested in was just about in focus, and he enhanced that section of the image. It sprang to glowing life in the air.

The door opened and a young girl in hideous clothing stepped out. She looked at the hidden camera for a second and Devon ordered, "Freeze frame!" He studied the picture of the girl. She had long dark hair — obviously she wasn't worried about somebody getting a sample. And in a way she was rather attractive.

It was almost a shame that he'd have to get rid of her.

"Hard copies," he ordered. "A dozen."

As his Terminal was working, everything suddenly went blank. Devon would have been worried if he hadn't seen this happen a number of times before. Since he knew what was causing it, he wasn't worried.

He was much closer to *terrified*.

WHAT HAVE YOU DONE?

The words of burning fire hung in the air, casting a reddish glow over him. The sentence hung there, accusatory. Devon had known this would happen, but there was no way he could have prepared for it. He felt sick to his stomach but he forced himself to answer.

I DID NOTHING, MALEFACTOR, he typed back on the speed-board. Malefactor refused to talk to Devon; he had *never* spoken to Devon. In fact, Devon didn't actually know that the Malefactor was even a man; Devon had decided simply to think of him that way for convenience.

The Malefactor had raised him, had given Devon everything that he possessed. This place to live, the Terminal, all the on-line access he ever needed (completely untraceable), and the freedom to do whatever Devon wished. In return, the Malefactor had taught Devon almost daily for years, until Devon had managed to outpace even the Malefactor's computer skills. Now the contacts between them might be as long as a week apart. It didn't bother Devon, because the Malefactor was the one person in the world who scared him.

The Malefactor knew all of Devon's secrets. And try as he had, Devon knew *nothing* about his mysterious benefactor and guardian. Except that when he gave orders, he expected them to be obeyed. And he had expressly forbidden the use of the Doomsday Virus beyond the test Devon had already run.

YOU HAVE MOVED PREMATURELY, the flaming words accused him.

"The program was initiated while I was off-line," Devon insisted. "It must have been a hacker. I'm trying to trace the person now."

There was a slight pause, and then: I KNOW. I HAVE BEEN MONITORING YOUR ACTIV-ITIES.

So — now Devon knew. He shivered. He'd always suspected that he was being monitored, but he'd never had any proof — until now. The Malefactor didn't trust him.

Smart decision.

Still, there was no way that even the Malefactor could read what Devon was thinking.

UPGRADE YOUR SECURITY ON THE QUIETUS ACCOUNT, the Malefactor ordered him. DO NOT LET THIS HAPPEN AGAIN.

Devon flushed. He was being scolded, as if he were a child like those in the family he monitored from time to time. Someone too stupid to think for himself, who constantly needed to be told what to do. Devon wanted to snarl back that he *knew* this must be done. But it wouldn't be wise to argue with the Malefactor — at least not until he knew what and who he was actually up against.

Besides, he hadn't actually thought about changing the security yet. He'd been obsessing on catching the hacker. I UNDERSTAND, he typed. I'LL TAKE CARE OF IT. But the anger smoldered inside him.

YOU'D BETTER, the burning words read in the air.

That was a threat. Definitely a threat. From a man he'd never met, a man who controlled Devon's life. With a start, Devon realized that he didn't even know what lay outside the walls of his compound. He'd never ventured beyond the front door. Where was the need, when he could have anything he wanted brought to him?

If the Malefactor cut him off, he'd be as helpless and lost as any of the peasants outside his little world.

I have to find a way to gain control of my own life, Devon thought. *I have to become stronger than the Malefactor. Otherwise I will never be safe.*

And the first step was to find this hacker and eliminate her from the game. He turned back to the photographs as his Terminal started up once more.

He had to plan this carefully.

9

ristan didn't know what to do. He couldn't access the Net without his account, and now that was gone. His hand-comp was too limited to be useful. That meant he was effectively cut off from the outside world. Even the Screen wouldn't work without his account. Luckily, the phone line was separate, or he wouldn't even have that link. But he had nothing else. All he could do was wait, and he hated to do that.

The phone chimed, startling him. Was it the shields already? Had they tracked him down? Steeling himself, he called, "Hello?"

Mora's image formed in front of him. "Hi, Tristan," she said. "Are you okay?"

"What do you mean?" He hadn't intended to sound sharp, but he was afraid that some of his guilt might have shown through.

"I was at school when I saw the news about your father's bank," she explained. "I canceled the school program immediately and called you. Is it true? Are you cut off?"

"Yes," Tristan said. "I can't access the Net, my money, or anything. I feel so . . . alone."

Mora smiled. "You want me to come over, so we can be alone together?" she suggested.

Tristan was surprised by his reaction to her question. Ordinarily, the idea of spending time alone with Mora would have thrilled him. But right now he just wanted to be by himself. He had to sort out his emotions and his responses. Besides which, he didn't want to involve Mora in any of the trouble he might be in.

He realized that he had to be alone in this. He would have to find out who he was by himself. He would have to decide what to do about the virus. He wanted to know who he was before committing Mora to be a part of him.

"I'm sorry, Mora," Tristan replied. "Not right now. Maybe later, okay? I've got some thinking to do."

Mora nodded, understanding, as she always did. "You know how to find me," she replied. "I'll be here." The phone cut off.

She'd be there, Tristan knew.

But where would *he* be?

Shimoda looked up from her desk, startled, as Peter Chen stormed into her office. Her boss had *never* been in here in person before, and he was clearly making a statement by slamming his way in now. "What's all this about?" he demanded furiously.

"A theft," Shimoda replied, composing herself. "Somebody robbed the First Security International Bank and then unleashed a killer virus that wiped the bank's computers clean to avoid being traced. The same virus was used in Buenos Aires earlier, on the airship, and against that house."

"And you have *no* information on this?" Chen cried.

"I'm working on it," Shimoda said patiently. "I couldn't track the culprit before the computer crashed at the bank. Which is probably a good thing if you think about it. Imagine what would have happened if that virus had latched onto my trace and ended up here. *Everything* could have been wiped."

"We have protection against such a thing," Chen protested.

"So did the bank," Shimoda responded dryly. "It kept the virus at bay for about a second."

This quietened Chen down a bit. "So how do you propose to trace this criminal?" he finally asked.

"Phone records," Shimoda explained. "I've got my Terminal tracking and logging everyone who calls in to complain that their accounts aren't accessible. We're then matching the calls against whoever was on-line when the bank crashed. If our crook stole money and is covering his or her tracks, then they have to complain to look good."

"An awful lot of people are going to complain," Chen answered. "The bank had tens of thousands of customers."

"And only eighty-four in the on-line area at the time," Shimoda said. "Some of whom are terrible with computers and can be eliminated immediately."

"But the person could have been using a false account," Chen protested. "If they are this good, it's possible."

"True," Shimoda agreed. "But I think they'd use their real account. They needed to be able to transfer the cash they stole to another account. So I then look for a DNA match to the first account. If there is one . . . that's an almost dead giveaway." She glanced at the computer screen. "So far there's just one name that stands out. A kid named Tristan Connor."

"Connor?" Chen looked worried. "There's a vice president of the bank named Connor."

"This is his son," Shimoda said. "And if we're looking for somebody who might have access to the coding needed to rob the bank blind, Tristan Connor is starting to look like a very good suspect."

"Yes," Chen agreed, rubbing his chin thoughtfully. "But none of this is proof."

"Not yet," Shimoda agreed. "But you have to admit, it's very good circumstantial evidence, isn't it? I think it's enough for me to go around and talk to the boy. I can disguise the purpose by pretending I want to talk to his father about the problem. If young Tristan is involved, I think his responses should be pretty interesting."

Chen considered her plan and then nodded. "His father is very important, though, so handle him with kid gloves. But if you find anything suggestive, I'll get a warrant, and we'll bring the boy in for questioning."

"Fine." Shimoda nodded and headed for the door.

Behind her, Chen tapped in a request for a flitter, which would be waiting by the street door when she reached it.

It was time to talk to Tristan Connor and see what he knew.

Devon tapped the photo against his keyboard, lost in thought. If this girl hacker was as good as she seemed to be, then she might make a perfect assistant for when he was ready for the big event. The problem with being as brilliant as he was, Devon reflected, was that it meant he had to do everything, and couldn't delegate. It would be nice to have help. But he needed to see just how clever she managed to be.

He bent to the speedboard and accessed one of his special cloaking devices. The idea of this program was to make his actions unmonitorable. Hopefully, he would be able to hide what he found from the Malefactor.

Hopefully.

"Terminal," he ordered. "Run a Net scan for any accounts with my DNA. Ignore your own, of course."

"Working," the Terminal said. A moment later, it added, "One match found."

Devon grinned to himself. So the little witch *had* been stealing from him! Somehow she'd managed to get a copy of his DNA and had replicated an IC. He was starting to admire her. "Details," he ordered. The Screen started to fill with the information and he scowled.

She'd invented a completely fake life, it seemed. Some kid named Tristan Connor. She'd somehow inserted a lot of stuff into his account. It looked absolutely genuine, too. He couldn't see a thing wrong with the information. She'd given him parents, a home address, a real life. There were records of activity and —

What?

Devon scowled and stared at the screen.

"Tristan Connor" had apparently been registered online when the bank had crashed. This was a stupid mistake for the hacker to make . . . and she didn't seem to be a stupid person. Devon's stomach started to ache, which was never a good sign. "Terminal," he ordered. "Access records for Tristan Connor. Check his address."

"It is listed to a Rojer Connor," the computer replied. "Vice president with First Security International Bank."

Surely the hacker never would have created a fake person who was supposed to be the son of one of the big guys in the bank she'd robbed?

Devon was *definitely* getting a bad feeling about this.

"Get me a visual on this Tristan Connor," he ordered.

A picture came up immediately. Devon saw it and almost stopped breathing.

It was *him* — Devon. How in Hades had this girl managed to get a picture of *him*? He never left the secured area here, and he'd *never* had his image taken. He was certain of that. And yet, there it was: definitely a picture of him. The same dark hair, the same dark eyes . . . How had she managed this? And more to the point, *why* had she done it?

Anybody checking the bank was bound to find this information. Had the girl deliberately left a trail to him to get him into trouble? Devon was sweating now. It was starting to look as if the girl not only knew about him, but was deliberately trying to get him blamed for what she'd done.

Unless . . .

"Terminal, check Rojer Connor's file," he ordered. "Does he have any children?"

"One," the Terminal responded. "A son. Tristan."

Devon bent to his speedboard, throwing the girl's photo to the floor as he typed. He checked, and then rechecked. It was no mistake. Connor did have a son. And the computer records insisted that it was Devon . . .

"I need some outside proof," he muttered. "Terminal, access the newsweb. Are there any pictures of Tristan Connor in the records?"

"Searching," the Terminal replied.

Devon was losing his cool. *This can't be happening,* he thought. It didn't make sense. If what this was starting to look like *was* true, then —

He didn't want to even *think* about that!

Devon was trying to keep a grip on his emotions, and for the first time in his life he was failing. There had to be *some* other explanation for this. . . .

"One image located," his Terminal reported.

Devon swallowed, building up his nerve. "Display it."

The image had been taken at some sort of school ceremony a few months ago. Tristan Connor was shown arm in arm with a tall, pretty blond girl. Devon's sweat turned to ice water. This was no longer a simple matter of the girl at the bank framing him.

Tristan Connor wasn't a fake account made up to frame Devon.

Tristan Connor was *real*.

And he was Devon's twin, right down to his DNA.

Devon closed his eyes and started to massage his aching temples. This was totally impossible. No two people's DNA matched exactly. Not parents and children. Not brothers and sisters. There was always some difference.

But the computer records insisted that Devon's and Tristan's DNA matched exactly. Then it was *Tristan* who had accessed and set off the Doomsday Virus, not the girl. She was just some almost-innocent bystander. *Almost* because she was definitely a crook; she'd faked Betti Cartmel's IC.

So . . . who was Tristan Connor, and why did he look so much like Devon?

"No!" Devon snapped. Tristan *couldn't* exist because he, Devon, was unique. There weren't two of him!

Except, apparently, there were.

Normally the one thing that could calm Devon down was a seascape with music. He yelled out for the Terminal to begin his Debussy program. The strains of *La Mer* wafted across the room, along with images of a tropical coral reef. Fish flitted around his head. Normally he found this very soothing.

Today it made him tense. "Off!" he screamed, trying to regain some semblance of control. His one power, the one thing made him superior to the rest of the human race, more worthy, more brilliant, was his DNA and his expertise with computers. It was what Quietus needed him for. But it looked like the Malefactor could have the same thing from Tristan Connor. *If* he knew that Tristan existed.

If he hadn't *made* Tristan exist, as he had created Devon.

Maybe it was time for Tristan to stop existing.

Devon considered his next move very carefully. The girl at the bank was a false lead, obviously. But the Malefactor didn't know that. Hopefully, he thought she was the guilty person and he was going to go after her. It would keep the Malefactor occupied and away from the *real* problem.

Which was perfect. Devon smiled to himself. The girl would make an excellent pawn to keep the Malefactor off the right track and happy. Let him have her; it didn't bother Devon. Such things never bothered Devon. She was just some crook, not worth leaving alive anyway. And to think he'd been almost ready to make her his assistant! That would have been a bad mistake.

While the girl was being dealt with, he'd work on Tristan Connor. First, he'd have to find out what was going on. Then he'd dispose of Tristan so that no one would ever know the truth. Devon would remain unique and indispensable . . . which was how it should be.

Devon downloaded Tristan's address and then contacted a team of security men. They were the only ones he could trust for this job. They were loyal to him because he could destroy them if he wished. After all, he had helped to make them. They knew this, and stayed on his good side. He rewarded them well, and they knew what would happen if he ever got annoyed with them. They made certain that he never did.

They were the ones to send after Tristan. Devon would find out what was going on . . . and then he would destroy his double.

Tristan felt confined in his silent, cut-off house. His parents had left, unable to work since they couldn't log on. They had gone to a neighbor's to try and find out what was happening on their Screens. Tristan didn't want to be around when they returned. The best solution, he realized, was to take a walk. He stepped out of the dead house and into the street. Naturally, nobody else was around. They were either working or on the Net. The children would be studying, of course, which is what Tristan should have been doing. But he was a straight-A student, and allowed to take time off because of it. Besides, since Tristan couldn't log on, he couldn't go to school, could he?

Unlike many people, Tristan normally enjoyed being outside. He liked to feel and experience things physically. But today wasn't normal, and he was rather afraid that any experiences coming to him would be all too real for his liking. He deserved to be punished, didn't he? He had broken into Control, and he had set that virus free. True, he'd managed to stop it, but it had destroyed a lot of people's lives. Tristan didn't know whether it would ever be possible to make up for that.

Should he go to a communications link somewhere, call the shields and give himself up? It would be the honest thing to do. And he'd always been brought up to be scrupulously honest . . .

. . . by people who'd lied to him all his life.

Tristan didn't know what to do. Yesterday, everything had seemed so obvious and clear. Today . . . today he was in a swamp of uncertainty, being dragged out of his depth.

He hadn't meant any harm, even though harm had been done. He had only been seeking the truth, even if he'd done it by lying about himself.

The ends justify the means? But he'd never believed that. Tristan had always been sure that the means justified the end. You couldn't create good by doing evil. You could only get at the truth by being truthful.

Or so he had thought. Now he just didn't know.

Where had all of his certainty, his moral core, gone? Could he ever get it back again?

He found himself standing beside a statue. It was about five meters tall, a man in an old-time fighting costume, carrying a laser rifle. TO THE HEROES OF THE BALKAN WAR, 2021, a small plaque read. Tristan knew about the war from his history classes, of course — a muddled conflict, with no real resolution. "Did you know what you were fighting for?" he asked the statue quietly. "Because, right now, I'm not sure I do." But he *had* to fight. If he surrendered to the shields, he'd be sent to jail. He'd be able to find out nothing there.

Even if it went against what he had been taught, he couldn't give himself up. Finding out who he was overrode everything else right now. He had to know the truth, no matter what. Removing his glove, he touched the words on the plaque, and then turned to head home again.

There was a small flitter moving down the street toward him. Tristan scowled as he watched it. Why would anybody be coming here physically? It was rather unusual. And even if it was paranoid, this bothered him. He started back toward his house.

The flitter sped up. Tristan glanced back and saw that

it was getting closer. Inside were three men, and they all had something in their hands. The shields? Had they traced him already? How? Tristan wasn't sure what to do. Run for it? But that would be like admitting his guilt.

The flitter drew level with him, and then sighed to a halt. Two of the men hopped lightly from the vehicle, blocking Tristan's path. Both held small guns. Tristan wasn't very familiar with weapons, but he recognized them as tazers, which would throw a small electrical charge. It wouldn't kill, but it would be very, very painful.

"Into the car," the first man said. He was a stocky character, who looked as if he'd retired from playing pro football only a week ago.

"Am I being arrested?" asked Tristan. "If so, on what charge?"

"Arrested?" The second man barked a laugh. He was taller and skinnier, and wore mirror shades so his eyes were invisible. "No, you jerk — you're being kid-napped."

Tristan had been worried before; now he was stunned and scared. Kidnapped? "What's going on?" he demanded.

"This isn't a lecture," the second man said. He gestured with his tazer. "Get into the flitter, or I'll fry your

122

nerves and then shove your twitching body in. It's your choice."

Tristan realized that the man was dead serious. "All right," he agreed, shaking slightly. He knew that he had no option. These men were professionals, that was clear. Both were armed, as was the driver. He didn't stand a chance of resisting. He started to move toward the vehicle . . . when the whole world seemed to explode.

The heavyset man gave a howl of pain, and spun around. There was a burn across his shoulder, and his tazer went flying. Tristan was overwhelmed by the stench of ozone, and then sensed another person running toward the group. The second man was whirling to fire at the approaching person. Seizing his chance, Tristan threw himself at the man.

The kidnapper was torn between two targets and reacted very slowly. Tristan managed to tackle him. Angry, the man slammed the barrel of his tazer across Tristan's neck. Tristan felt a sudden surge of pain and his vision blurred. He fell to his knees, and was unable to rise. He looked up and saw the weapon being aimed at him.

Facing capture, Tristan managed to find a small reserve of energy. He lunged forward, raking his fingers across his attacker's hand and drawing bloody welts. The man cursed and drew his hand back without shooting.

"Into the flitter!" the driver yelled. "Now!"

The second man didn't hesitate. He threw himself inside. The heavy man, nursing his injured shoulder, was already there. The driver accelerated the flitter to top speed. It sped down the road as the person who'd saved Tristan arrived, panting, and took one final, futile shot after it. Then she swore.

Tristan's vision was starting to clear. He looked up at a petite Asian woman in a pale blue suit. She was holding her gun at the ready and breathing heavily. "Thank you," he managed to say. "You saved me from being kidnapped."

"It's my job," the woman informed him. "I have some questions for you, Tristan Connor, and you couldn't answer them if you were kidnapped. My name is Inspector Taki Shimoda, of the Computer Control Police. Shall we go inside and talk?"

Tristan paled. It looked as if all of his circuits were fried now. . . .

10

The inspector activated her wrist phone as she helped Tristan back to the Connor house.

"Inspector Shimoda," she announced as Tristan watched her. "Priority alert. I want a trace on a flitter heading north from my location. Three men."

There was a slight pause and then the shield Terminal announced, "There are no flitters currently in operation within four kilometers of your location."

"That's impossible," Shimoda said. Tristan could hear the anger in her voice. "There's one within a kilometer or so. I want all IC tracers that are moving to be displayed."

"There are no tracers currently moving faster than walking speed," the Terminal replied.

That made no sense to Tristan. He'd *seen* three men, and the Terminal should be able to track them for the police. And the vehicle, too.

"Damn." Shimoda glared and then turned to face Tristan. "Well, it looks as if your playmates are shielded somehow. Just who were those men?"

"I don't know," Tristan answered honestly. "I was out for a walk and they tried to kidnap me."

"Why?"

"They didn't say." Tristan swallowed.

Shimoda nodded. "It's a crazy crime," she muttered. "Even if we couldn't trace them, we could trace *you*. It doesn't make any sense." She put her gun away finally, and her eyes focused on Tristan's hand. "You scratched one of them?"

Tristan looked at his fingernails, stained with the blood he'd drawn. "Yes," he said, with a satisfaction that was almost brutal. It surprised him. He was amazed, too, that he'd taken off his glove and forgotten to replace it. He usually did such things without even thinking about them. Obviously, it had to be the result of the shock he'd experienced, that he hadn't even noticed.

Shimoda finally grinned, which made her look less policelike and actually quite pretty. "But it gives me a DNA sample to work with." She bent over Tristan's hand, using a probe to scrape blood and skin from under his nails. This she slipped into a sample pouch, and then crossed to Tristan's Terminal.

"It's not on," Tristan told her. "Something happened at the bank." He hoped he sounded innocent, but he suspected it was rather pointless. It was obvious that Shimoda hadn't simply been passing by. She had said she wanted to talk to him.

"*Your* account is down," she agreed. "But mine isn't." She tapped at commands, keeping what she was doing hidden from them both. A moment later, the Screen came to life with the face of a policeman. "I want you to check on this DNA sample," Shimoda ordered, placing a portion on the scanner. "Check it out, and find out who it belongs to. Then get a warrant for his arrest. The charges are attempted kidnapping, resisting arrest, and cloaking his IC." Tristan knew that the third charge was probably the one carrying the stiffest penalty.

"Understood." The policeman vanished.

The inspector turned back to Tristan. She was scowling, but obviously puzzled. "You've no idea why those men wanted to kidnap you?" she asked.

"None at all," Tristan said honestly. "I was just out . . . walking."

"Your father is a bank vice president. Maybe they thought he'd pay a ransom to get you back?" Shimoda suggested.

That was a possible idea, he knew, even if it was really far-fetched. "But the bank's out of commission," he protested. "Dad can't get at his money."

"Nobody at the bank can," Shimoda agreed. "It's chaos there right now. But those men may not have known that. Anyway, the bank problem is what I wanted to talk to you about. According to the records, you were on-line at the time the virus struck. Did you notice anything odd?"

Tristan swallowed again, hoping he could keep his voice steady without being obvious. "Aside from the bank suddenly dying, you mean?" He shook his head. "I was just doing some schoolwork, and then the whole thing went dead."

"I see." Shimoda's eyes narrowed. "You noticed nothing unusual, then?"

"No." He frowned, trying to look innocent. "Why are you questioning me?"

"We're questioning everyone who was on-line at the time," the inspector said. "We're trying to discover what caused this problem."

"Do you think the bank problem and this kidnapping might be connected?" asked Tristan.

"It's hard to say," Shimoda replied after a moment. "But I'd advise you to be very careful. Does this house have security systems?"

"Yes," Tristan confirmed. Then he winced. "But they're probably tied in through the Net. That means that they'll be down now."

The policewoman nodded. "That makes sense." She looked at them both. Tristan couldn't tell if she believed his story as she was carefully giving nothing away. "Well, I can't leave you here without protection. Do you want to come to Computer Central with me? We could guard you there."

"I could go to my girlfriend's house," Tristan counteroffered. He didn't want to go to a shield station for any reason. Aside from the fact that it would feel too much like he was under arrest, he'd certainly be watched. Which meant that he wouldn't be able to do his own investigating, his priority right now. "That's secure."

"Okay," the inspector agreed. "You'd better tell me the address, in case I need to contact you. Can you tell your parents to stay away from the house, too, for now? If this was a kidnapping for money, the crooks might target them next."

"No problem," Tristan said. "They're at a neighbor's house right now. Maybe they could stay there. Could I have you make the call?" He gestured to his own phone. "I can receive calls, but dialing out is kind of difficult without the Terminal."

"No problem." Shimoda made the call and warned Tristan's parents to stay where they were. Neither argued, though his mother asked where Tristan was. She seemed relieved to hear he was going to stay with Mora's family for the time being.

When Shimoda had finished, Tristan cleared his throat. "Uh, do you have any idea how long it will be until our credit is restored and we can go back to normal?"

"None at all," Shimoda admitted. "This kind of thing has never happened before, and there's a lot of panic over it. Whoever is responsible is going to be facing a very long, stiff jail sentence. It's wrecked the lives of thousands of people."

Tristan winced from the guilt he felt. "Including mine," he said, trying to cover for his reaction. "I haven't been able to get on the Net for hours."

"Yes, well, there are thousands like you," she answered, not showing much sympathy. "It's one big mess, and it's going to take a while to figure it out." She shrugged. "Well, I'll give you a ride to your girlfriend's home in my flitter. Just pack a few clothes, I guess. Hopefully, this will be sorted out soon. That DNA sample should tell us who we're looking for very shortly."

Tristan nodded, and hurried upstairs to his room. His hands were shaking as he packed his bag. If Shimoda found out he was responsible for the bank's crash, she'd lock him away forever, by the sound of it. . . .

His stomach hurt almost as much as his conscience.

Devon sat and fumed. He needed to find out more about this Tristan Connor, and so far he'd struck out. Those idiot thugs of his had messed up their kidnapping attempt and let Tristan escape — into the hands of a shield, yet! A very poor move indeed, which complicated the game. And, thanks to the bank computer having crashed, Tristan's house was without Net capacity. Devon had attempted to access the Connor security system, but it was totally dead. He couldn't even watch his twin. Another bad move.

Sighing, Devon got to his feet and strode the confines of his Terminal room. Okay, so two moves had failed him. But he was the master player here, and a couple of fouled-up moves wouldn't mean the end of his game. There was always another brilliant move possible. . . . He just had to think of it.

That image of Tristan . . . He had the Terminal recall it. His double was with a pretty blond girl. "Identify the girl in this image," he ordered.

"Her name is Mora Worth," his Terminal responded.

"Locate her residence," Devon ordered. He grinned to himself. The ordinary people of the world liked to have emotional entanglements with the opposite sex, he knew. He wasn't interested, of course. For one thing, there wasn't a girl in the world intelligent enough to be worth spending time with. For another, getting emotionally involved with a fragile person would complicate his life and undoubtedly irritate him. But though Tristan *looked* like him, he couldn't possibly *act* like him or be as smart as he was. For one thing, he had this girl.

A weakness that Devon could use. Tristan was bound to go and see her sometime. It was part of human weakness to want to share with others. And when Tristan went to see her, Devon would have him again. "Tie into the security monitors at her home," he ordered his Terminal.

The Screen lit up, showing a split shot through each monitor in the house. There was a roof garden with one of those asinine Pegasus Ponies grazing there; a kitchen, currently empty of life; and then four rooms with people in them. Two were parents, obviously telecommuting; he shut those monitors down. One was a younger girl, apparently at school. Boring; that went as well. That left Mora herself, on the comm unit chatting to someone. He flagged that one.

"Follow that girl if she moves anywhere," he ordered the Terminal. Then he highlighted the final Screen, showing the front approach to the house. "And monitor this one, too. If Tristan Connor shows up, alert me instantly, as a priority override."

"Understood," the Terminal answered.

Right, that was the next move planned. Devon might have to wait awhile, but he was certain this would hook him Tristan again. Meanwhile, there was still a lot of work to do. He needed to know just who Tristan Connor was, and why he had been created. The only person who could probably give him answers was the Malefactor, but Devon knew that there was no point in asking him anything. In the first place, the Malefactor might not know about Tristan. In that case, Devon didn't want to alert the man. It was better that he never knew. On the other hand, Tristan might be some sort of a secret weapon of the Malefactor's. In that event, Devon didn't want the Malefactor to know that he knew about Tristan.

Devon wasn't entirely sure how big an organization Quietus was. He knew it had tentacles throughout the power structure of the world, but he didn't know who its members might be, or how many there were. It might be a tiny group, or it could be thousands of people. He'd never bothered to find out. After all, he was their secret weapon. He was the one who had developed the Doomsday Virus, and they couldn't use it without him.

Except, of course, now they could. *Tristan* could launch it.

Was that the Malefactor's plan? Had he simply been using Devon all along, having him develop the virus, with the aim of killing him off and replacing him with the more controllable Tristan? Perhaps, perhaps not. Devon didn't know. But there was a way to solve the problem — by disposing of Tristan so that there wasn't a backup possibility, if that was the plan.

Tristan was, of course, a clone of Devon. His birth records showed that he'd been born a week after Devon himself. Somebody — the Malefactor was still the best suspect — must have taken a cell sample from Devon and used it to clone Tristan. And then Tristan had been hidden away, raised by some dupes somewhere. A secret weapon, waiting to be activated . . .

Well, Quietus, the Malefactor, or whoever else was responsible for this farce was going to discover just how efficient a player Devon was. Tristan would have to vanish, utterly. There would be no replacement for Devon, if that was the plan.

And if it wasn't? If there was some other reason why Tristan had been created? Well, who cared? Disposing of him was logically the only thing to do.

Genia walked through the dark, smelly streets of the Underworld, grinning to herself. The chip she held was her key to a fortune . . . if she used it properly. No more having to rob people and chance getting caught. Again, she realized she might make enough money from this fragment of the virus to move Above.

She had to wonder about that though. Not that she'd mind leaving these disgusting and sometimes dangerous streets, of course. To have a home where you could see the sun anytime you felt like it! To be able to mingle with people who were actually worth talking to. Maybe even to have friends for the first time in her life . . . All of those things would be great.

And maybe she'd be able to have a boyfriend. That sounded like it could be fun. She'd read about such things in her books, and she wondered what it would be like to be kissed, to be held in some guy's arms . . . The heroines in the books all seemed to think it was the greatest thing in the world. Personally, she thought it was kind of silly. To let some guy stick his lips on yours! It sounded more like something to laugh at than to want. But she wasn't going to knock it until she'd had a chance to try it.

But there were drawbacks, too. She'd have to get an IC. She'd have a real life, one she'd have to guard from people like herself. And she'd have to mix with respectable folk, the people she'd robbed all of her life.

Genia's thoughts were broken by a noise behind her. She wasn't entirely sure what she'd heard, but it had been something moving. It sounded like something large. She whirled around but there was nothing visible. Only lakes of shadows. Genia tried to dismiss the sound. The buildings were all decaying, after all, and it might just have been some bricks falling loose.

Or it might be the Tabat . . .

Genia stared at the buildings, but there was nothing moving, and no further noise. Maybe she was just getting jumpy. Maybe she really did need to go Above and put all of this behind her. Shrugging, she set off again toward her apartment.

There was another sound — definitely movement, not the buildings settling. She whirled around, staring back. Again, she saw nothing.

"Who's there?" she called, reaching into her bag for her tazer. "Come on out. I heard you."

Nothing. But she *knew* there was someone or something out there.

What if it was the Tabat?

Genia started to walk again, slowly, her hand on the gun. Her eyes flickered back and forth, searching the shadows for whatever was after her. She paused, her heart pounding. Had she seen a quick movement in one doorway? Or was she just trying too hard? She focused as clearly as she could and took another step. . . .

There was a sound behind her, and she whirled

around again. Two men had moved from the shadows, their hands clutching what had to be weapons. They weren't hungry scavengers. Both men wore dark suits and hats, with shades — down here in the shadows! — so that she couldn't tell much about them. But they clearly had money, and they didn't need whatever she had to offer. Yet they were rushing her.

Genia dropped her bag, bringing up her tazer and firing. The first man grunted and fell to his knee. Genia was startled; he should have been writhing on the floor in agony, hardly able to breathe. She figured he had to be wearing some sort of shielding — which was supposed to be impossible — or else he was very, very tough.

The second man fired back. Genia screamed as her hand became a flame of pain. The tazer clattered from her fingers and she cried in agony, tears running down her face. Even so, she wasn't about to stand still and be caught — or worse.

She started to run, deciding that it was time to kick her pride into the gutter. She couldn't fight two men who could shrug off tazer fire and who looked like they would be able to rip her apart with their bare hands. It was time to head for her apartment and the better defenses there.

The man on his feet changed course and slammed into her. Genia's breath was knocked out of her body and she crashed into the sidewalk. She howled again as her left side burned with pain. A broken brick gashed across her shoulder. Her attacker whacked her on the side of the head with the barrel of his tazer. Her head rang, but she hardly felt the extra pain. Her whole body hurt right now, and blood was leaking over her clothes from her injured shoulder.

"You'd better not fight anymore," the man growled. "I was told to bring you in, but Quietus will take you if you're damaged. Stay still or I'll break something. Maybe one of your wrists. Maybe an ankle. It depends on what mood I'm in." She could tell from his tone that he wasn't bluffing.

And she knew she'd made a terrible mistake taking that virus. Whoever had created it knew she had it. And he intended to make sure she never used it. The two thugs were probably ordered to bring her in for questioning. Then she'd be killed. There would be no money for her, no soft life.

In fact, no life at all.

It hadn't been the Tabat after her. But it was something just as deadly.

The man moved to check on his friend, and Genia

managed to sit up. Her shoulder was a mass of pain and blood, and her side hurt bad. Her right hand was useless, but at least the agony inside it was dying away. Her head hurt, but she could still think and see straight.

The two men moved back toward her, their tazers at the ready. The man she'd hit had lost his shades and she could see the pure evil in his eyes. Whatever this Quietus was, these two were thugs, pure and simple. They were going to take her in, and she knew that it would be a long and painful trip. These men enjoyed hurting people.

Genia didn't want to give up, but she couldn't see any way out of this one.

And then *something* moved from the shadows. Genia couldn't see exactly what it was, just that it was *big*. Two long, hairy arms reached out, wrapping around the shadeless man. He gave a cry as he was jerked from his feet and hauled into the shadows. There was a short, loud cracking sound and then the man fell to the ground, his back bent at an unnatural angle.

Genia choked back a scream. She'd been right after all! The Tabat was real. . . .

And it was a killer.

The second man turned around and fired at the

shape in the shadows. Tazer fire illuminated something. Genia could see claws and fangs, and two burning yellow eyes. Howling, the creature snatched at the man and bit downward at his neck.

As the dying man screamed, Genia got to her feet and ran. Her side was on fire and she staggered as she moved, but she didn't look back and she wouldn't give in to her weakness. To do so would be to die. Fighting off the nausea and the pain, she forced herself to run away from the site. Behind, she heard the thing tearing the man's body apart, and knew that if it came after her she'd suffer the same fate. She didn't dare falter.

And then her hotel was ahead of her. She pushed through the doors and hurried to the stairs. Her side ached badly and her blouse was soaked in blood. She felt weak and sick, but she couldn't stop here. Staggering up the stairs she almost fainted. Only her willpower kept her going. She reached the landing facing her apartment, and the security system focused on her. Recognizing her, it allowed her to pass. If the Tabat followed, it wouldn't be as lucky. It might not be stopped by tazers, but these security lasers would fry its flesh on the bones. It didn't matter how strong it was, it would die before it reached her door.

She hoped.

She made it to the keypad and pressed her hand against it. The door sighed open and she staggered inside. Leaning against the wall, she locked the door, keeping the security system primed. A wave of nausea washed over her and she managed to hobble to the bathroom. She threw up in the toilet, then washed out her mouth.

Genia knew she couldn't stay here like this. Forcing herself back to her feet, she peeled off her top. She almost screamed as it pulled free of her shoulder. She tossed the ruined rag aside and looked down at the wound. It was about four inches long and still bleeding. The edges were raw, and it hurt like the devil had stuck his pitchfork in her and was twirling it around. She opened the medicine cabinet. Her right hand was starting to return to normal, but she had to try three times to get it to apply the bacterial spray on her cut. Then she took a sponge and gently cleaned the wound. That hurt like anything, but she was finally able to slap on a regenerative bandage. The painkiller lining started to take effect, and she could take a breath at last without sending sharp pains through her shoulder.

She took stock of the rest of her injuries. Down her left side, her skin was raw from where she'd hit the sidewalk. There was a lump across her head where she'd been hit with the gun. And there was a bruise forming across the bottom of her spine, leading under the belt of her skirt. It was going to be tough sitting down for a while.

But at least she was alive to feel the pain. Genia was shaking from what she had witnessed. Not just the men, but the Tabat. It had been after her but had settled for her attackers instead.

She wasn't safe here any longer. She had to get out. Those men had been looking for her, and she had to assume that once they failed to report in there would be others.

Obviously her first plan, buying freedom with the virus, wasn't going to work. She had to fall back now on plan B — contacting the shields. It wouldn't make her rich, but maybe it would keep her alive.

Shaking, Genia pulled on a very loose top to avoid aggravating her injuries. Then she headed for her phone. She had to get help, and get it fast.

11

Devon watched his Screen avidly. His deductions had been correct: the monitors at the Worth house had picked up Tristan and that policewoman approaching in her flitter. Devon observed as Tristan climbed out and spoke a few words to the woman. The flitter then drove off, as Tristan headed toward the house.

But as soon as the flitter was gone from sight, Tristan turned away.

Interesting. Devon grinned. Tristan obviously had something in mind, and Devon was sure he knew what it was: He was going to return to his own home, where he felt safe enough. His clone seemed to be intent on doing something without being observed, even by his girlfriend.

That was *really* cooperative of him, doing just what Devon wanted.

It was almost too simple, really. Tristan might be his clone, Devon mused, but he didn't have Devon's intelligence. Well, not too much of it. He was so predictable. And foolish. With a laugh, Devon set to work. The hardest part would be bugging Tristan's Terminal in a way that Tristan wouldn't suspect.

It took Devon all of two minutes to do *that* little trick.

Devon grinned as he studied his speedboard. *Come into my parlor, said the spider to the fly. . . .*

Shimoda was driving the flitter back to her office, lost in thought. It was a good thing that the flitters were controlled by Traffic Terminals, because she wasn't paying attention to the road at all. All she could think about was Tristan Connor. Every instinct she had as a police officer told her that he was covering up something.

The kidnapping attempt had surprised her. It was lucky that she'd arrived in time to foil it, but what had caused it? There was clearly a lot more to this case than there had first seemed. Those thugs had some-how evaded the computer search, and their flitter had been shielded. They weren't simply opportunists who had decided to kidnap a banker's son for ransom. There was much more to it — but what? And how could they have evaded Control's monitors?

Her wrist-comp chimed, and the duty officer's face appeared. "The DNA trace has been completed," he said formally. Shimoda frowned because he looked very stiff and annoyed.

"About time," she grumbled. "Have you issued a war-rant and tracked the man down?"

"No and yes," the officer answered, his face unread-able. "There will be no warrant, and he has been tracked."

"No warrant?" Shimoda glared at him in fury. "I saw him with my own eyes attempting to kidnap two people. Can you give me any good reason why I can't get a war-rant?"

"I can give you two," the officer replied. "First of all, you *couldn't* have seen this man doing anything stren-uous, because he's on serious medication. After all, he's ninety years old."

"What?" Shimoda stared at her screen in utter con-fusion. "There must be some mistake," she protested.

"The man I saw couldn't have been more than thirty, and he was extremely fit."

"There's certainly been some mistake," agreed the duty officer. "The DNA sample you sent me belongs to Dennis Borden."

It took a moment for that to sink in. "Dennis Borden?" Shimoda repeated stupidly. "*The* Dennis Borden?"

"The *the* himself," the policeman agreed. "Senior Vice President Dennis Borden. Your boss and mine. And that's the second reason why there's no warrant — he's hardly likely to authorize his own arrest, is he?"

Shimoda was absolutely lost here. The ground had slipped from beneath her feet, and she was sinking fast. This didn't make any sense at all. "I don't understand," she said dully. "There has to have been an error."

"There hasn't been any error," the man replied. "I've run the checks myself three times. That's what took so long. Somehow, Inspector, you must have been fooled. That can't have been Borden's DNA."

But *how*? She had seen Tristan scratch the man with her own eyes. Then she had taken the sample herself from the boy's fingernails and sent it in. *How* could she have been fooled? Was it possible that Tristan Connor was playing some elaborate game with her? That he had set the whole thing up to get her into trouble? Even granting such a wild theory, however could he have managed to get a DNA sample from one of the most securely guarded men on Earth? None of this was making sense, and Shimoda was afraid it was making less and less sense every minute she was on this case. Now what could she do?

"Thanks," she said slowly. "I guess that the sample must have been planted somehow. You'd better just shelve it. I don't think we need to report it further."

The officer's face relaxed. "My thoughts exactly. I'll just mark it *contaminated sample* and erase it from the records." He hesitated, as if he wanted to say more, and then broke the link.

Shimoda sat there, oblivious to the town she was passing through. What was going on? The man Tristan had clawed certainly couldn't have been Dennis Borden. He'd been way too young for that. Somebody must have interfered with her work. Maybe the duty officer had switched samples on her? It was clear that the men she was tracking had some powerful help somewhere, if they couldn't be tracked by computer and their flitter didn't show up in the register. Were there people in her own department working for the crooks? It made a sick sort of sense. On the other hand, what could such a conspiracy of corruption have to do with a computer virus and Tristan Connor?

There were simply too many questions, and way too few answers. The one thing she was certain of was that she couldn't file any accurate reports on this case yet. If there was somebody in the department who was covering something up, she couldn't take any chances.

Shimoda hated to do this. She was a team player, not a lone gunman. But in this case, she had very little choice. She still had some of the DNA sample left, and she could check it herself, given the right equipment and time. Then she'd be able to tell if the duty officer was lying or not.

Her wrist-comp chimed again. "There's a caller for you," an Operator Terminal said. "A young girl, asking for whoever is investigating the First Security International crash. We've traced the call to the Underworld."

The Underworld? This was getting more and more bizarre every minute.

"Okay," Shimoda decided. "Put the call through to me."

The Screen changed, and she was looking into the face of a girl — maybe sixteen years old — who was obviously very scared. "I'm Inspector Shimoda," the policewoman said gently. "You wanted to talk to me?"

"Yes," the girl answered. "I need you to meet me and take me to safety. There are people after me."

Shimoda shook her head. "You live in the Underworld. You must know I'm not allowed down there. I can't help you."

"You *have* to help me," the girl insisted. "I have a sample of the killer virus that destroyed the bank's computer. I was logged in at the time, and snared the sample. It might tell you who created it. But there's a price — you have to get me out of here and keep me safe."

The virus? Shimoda's heart raced. If the girl was telling the truth, then she might have the very clue she needed to crack this case open. But . . . the girl was from the Underworld, and those characters were smart, devious, and nasty.

"You're right," Shimoda admitted carefully. "I would like that sample." She bit at her lip as she considered everything. "But I can't come down to you. You know there would be a riot if the police were spotted down there. Can you come up to me?"

The girl looked scared at the thought, but she finally nodded. "Okay," she agreed. "I'll have to chance it, I guess. Can you meet me at Twelfth Street and Fourth Avenue in fifteen minutes? The bank Terminal there?"

Shimoda tapped the flitter's controls and pulled up a route map. "Twenty," she said. "I'm resetting my destination now."

"Okay," the girl said. "I'll see you then. I hope." She broke contact.

The flitter changed direction, heading for the rendezvous spot. Shimoda didn't know if this was genuine, but the fact that the girl had agreed to come Above suggested that it was. She'd been well dressed and groomed, and seemed to be very bright. And her fear had seemed genuine, too. If she was telling the truth, this could be Shimoda's biggest break yet. . . .

If the girl could be trusted.

12

Tristan reached home again without being spotted. Things were getting way too scary for him. That policewoman, Inspector Shimoda, had seemed to be nice enough, and her help had saved his hide. But he could tell that there was a lot of steel under the velvet veneer of her personality. She suspected something, and Tristan was sure she'd be around again soon. And then there were those thugs who had tried to kidnap him. . . .

Who did they work for? This Quietus he had been

warned about? Had his messing up alerted them to his existence? He knew he shouldn't return home again, since those men knew where he lived and might strike again. But, though the Worth house was safer, it might put Mora in peril. And he couldn't chance that.

Besides, now he had a way to get back on-line, thanks to the inspector.

Entering the house, he set the security zone to full intensity. If anyone tried to approach the house, it would go to full alert. The only people who could get through the zone now were his parents — and they were still at the neighbors'. So he should be undisturbed.

Tristan was feeling quite smug. Inspector Shimoda had bypassed the bank's wrecked lines and used what was probably a private police line. She undoubtedly felt that it was secure enough.

She was wrong.

Tristan powered up his Terminal and then ran one of his own special programs. He'd designed it to use on other machines, mostly as a joke. Running his search dog, he could discover what programs and Net services any other machine had been using within a day or so. It was fun to freak his friends out sometimes by telling them everything they'd been up to. He'd never imagined he'd find a serious use for it, until today. He set the search dog going inside his own Terminal, and waited for the results.

He couldn't suppress a smile at his own ingenuity when the answer came up. Using the same pattern Shimoda had, he accessed the shield web, gave a false name, hacked in a password, and he was on-line again. If anyone suspected anything and tried to trace it, it would show the user as Inspector Shimoda. It might be funny to see her try and explain *this* away! The chances were, though, that nobody would ever know he'd managed this.

Devon raised an eyebrow; his clone wasn't *quite* as stupid as he'd believed. Tristan had managed to get himself back on-line again, and in rather a clever fashion. Part of Devon's Terminal was showing him exactly what Tristan was up to. As Devon had suspected, he was looking for the Quietus account again. He was obviously trying to work out what was happening to him.

With a grin, Devon decided to be nice to his stupider self; it was time that the two of them had a little chat. . . .

But first, of course, he had to make absolutely certain they wouldn't be interrupted. Devon checked his

Terminal to see that Tristan had locked his house and set the security programs into operation. That was helpful of him, but it didn't make the house quite secure enough. The Connors could still get in.

Devon tapped in the command codes on his speedboard. His Terminal seized control of the security lockouts for the Connor house and changed them. *Nobody* could get in now.

Or out . . . unless Devon allowed it.

Tristan wasn't getting out alive.

Shimoda drew her flitter to a halt at the bank, and the girl hurried over to her. The girl was looking all around, obviously afraid she was being followed. Shimoda had scanned the area and was pretty sure she hadn't been. The girl slid into the seat beside Shimoda and gave a sigh of relief.

"Maybe we should go now?" she suggested.

Shimoda allowed the computer to take control, and the flitter slid smoothly out into the street. Then she turned to examine the youngster beside her. She was scared, that was obvious. But she was bright, well dressed — if in a rather tacky style that Shimoda didn't much like — and well fed. Not the average Underworld type, that was for certain.

"What's your name?" Shimoda asked.

"Do you need to know?" the girl asked in a hostile tone.

"No," Shimoda replied. "I could just call you Fred. But I'd feel better knowing your name if I'm going to help you. You *did* ask for my help, as I recall."

The girl considered this, and finally nodded. "Genia," she said.

"Right, Genia." Shimoda smiled, but it didn't have any noticeable effect on the girl. "As of now, you're in my protective custody. Until we figure out anything better, you stick to me like a glove. Understand?"

"No," Genia replied. "I've seen enough shields on my Screen to know that's not the normal way this is done."

"It isn't," Shimoda agreed. "But this isn't a normal case. To be honest, I'm not entirely sure who I can trust right now. Including you. So until I know who's on my side and who isn't, you stay with me. And if I think you're playing me for a fool, I'll have you locked away."

"You'd Ice me?" Genia squealed. "I thought you were going to *help* me. Save my life, that kind of thing."

"Trust me, you'd be very safe Iced." Taki smiled at the worried girl. "Now, what about this virus?"

Genia looked defiant, and then had second thoughts. She reached up her long sleeve and pulled out a chip.

"It's on here," she said. "Whoever designed it knows I've got it, and they tried to kill me to get it back."

"Ah." Shimoda took the chip and looked at it. "Nice work — programmable portable chip, huh? Quite a nifty piece of workmanship. And, of course, evidence against you."

"Now, wait a minute —"

Shimoda held up her hand. "But that's minor stuff compared to what I'm after. I'm not going to push it if you behave. But if you *don't* behave, you're going on Ice for a long, long time. Look, Genia — for all I know, *you* created this virus."

"Yeah, right, and then I tried to murder myself." Genia's eyes flashed with anger. "Are all shields as dumb as you, or did I just pick a loser?"

Shimoda glared at the girl. "Watch your mouth, kid. Anyone smart enough to make a killer virus might just be egotistical enough to try running a scam on me. But if you are, it won't work."

"And I thought *I* was paranoid," Genia muttered. "I'm really starting to think that trusting you was a mistake."

"It isn't, as long as you're honest," the policewoman informed her. "But you're going to have to convince me of that. So pardon me for being suspicious, but I can't help it." She looked at the chip. "We're heading to my apartment. I want to check out this virus, but not at Control."

"Why not?"

Shimoda wondered how much to tell the girl. If this was a scam, then she already knew the truth. If it wasn't, then it probably wouldn't hurt her to be informed. "I think somebody there is working with the crook or crooks," she explained. "And until I know who it is, I can't trust anybody."

"Oh, great." Genia slumped back in her seat. "In other words, I'm not only going to have to run from the bad guys, but some of the good guys might turn out to be bad guys, too?"

"Yes, that's about right," Shimoda agreed grimly.

"Stupid me. I thought the day couldn't get any worse. And it just has."

That, Shimoda realized, was probably true. But if the girl was right, the chip might hold what they needed to solve the case. *If* she was right.

At the moment, Shimoda didn't have any other hope.

Tristan was feeling rather pleased with himself . . . until the house suddenly went dark.

He whirled around, but he could see absolutely nothing. His Screen had died, the speedboard useless. The windows had polarized, blocking incoming light. He could hear the sound of the security program locking every door in the house.

What was going on? He hadn't ordered any of this. Had he triggered some kind of alarm at shield head-quarters, causing them to lock him down? He jumped to his feet, and yelped as he cracked his shin on the edge of his desk. Trying to ignore the sharp pain, he stumbled across his room to the window. Running his fingers around the edge, he found the polarization con-trols, but they were dead to his touch.

"You're so *embarrassing*, you know that?"

Tristan whirled around as he heard the voice issuing from his dead Terminal. Abruptly, there was light in his room again as a holographic image formed, standing between Tristan and the Terminal. Tristan stared as it filled in and fleshed out.

It was *his own face*. Not exactly, of course — the fig-ure was wearing a looser top and tighter pants, both in a sort of Day-Glo orange. And the hair was a bit wilder and a little longer. But the image was his own.

"What sort of a game is this?" Tristan demanded.

"*My* sort of game," the double answered, grinning. "My rules, my game, and my win. But you're welcome to try and play along if you like." The figure walked forward, peering at Tristan. "I was *very* curious to see you."

Tristan wasn't sure what was happening here. Someone outside his home had managed to seize control of his computer somehow. That much was obvious. How this person had done it, Tristan didn't have a clue. But if he could get to his speedboard, he might be able to overcome it.

"Who are you?" Tristan asked. "And why have you made yourself look like me?"

"Like *you*?" The figure laughed. "Wrong, dumbo. *You* look like *me*. And that's about the extent of our resemblance, thankfully. You don't have my brains, my style, or my charm." He stared at Tristan. "Or my dress sense."

Tristan didn't understand. "You're telling me that what I'm seeing isn't some sort of hologram projection?"

"Of course it is, you idiot. But it's a projection of *me*, not of *you*."

Shaking his head, Tristan inched forward. "That's not possible. I know there are a lot of stupid Screen shows that have evil-twin stories. But it never happens in real life. I don't have a twin."

The figure sighed. "You know, every time I start thinking we're just a teensy bit alike, you go and say something so stupid that I realize that appearances aren't everything. I'm not any kind of twin. *You're* my clone."

Tristan was stunned. He stared at the figure, and simply couldn't think.

A *clone* . . .

Devon walked around his darkened room. His Terminal was projecting his image into Tristan's room, and on his Screen was that room, including Tristan looking at him, absolutely speechless. Which was an improvement.

So this is my clone, Devon mused. The resemblance was uncanny. Tristan's hair was slightly shorter, and he was slightly skinnier than Devon. And he was dressed in dismal green. Other than that, Devon could have been looking at himself. It was only when Tristan opened his mouth that the differences between them became absolutely clear. Tristan was quite smart, of course, but he lacked Devon's brilliance.

It was a relief to Devon to know that he was still unique, despite this clone of his. They might have duplicated his body, but nobody could have duplicated his brilliance. His upbringing had been so careful, his education calculated to enhance his mind, his training precise to make him the computer maverick he had become. Tristan had some of Devon's potential, true enough, but he lacked all that made Devon essentially unique.

Plus, Tristan had a lot of unhealthy emotional baggage that wasn't weighing Devon down. That weakness for the girl, Mora, for one thing. And some strange ethical concerns about right and wrong. To Devon, there was only *strength* and *weakness*.

And Devon was strong, while Tristan was weak.

Tristan still could hardly believe what the stranger who looked almost exactly like him was claiming. In one day, he'd plunged from being the loved child of the Connors to, apparently, nothing but a clone of this gloating character. Was it possible?

Unfortunately, he didn't know. There was a heavy ache in his stomach as he considered the possibility. He was all too afraid that this person was right. It would explain a lot. If Tristan was a clone of this person, it would explain why there was another on-line account with his exact DNA that was not his. And that meant . . .

"Are you Quietus?" he asked the amused figure.

"Not as such, no," his double confessed. "Though we do have a lot in common. My name is Devon."

"And that Doomsday Virus I accidentally activated," Tristan said, working it out as he went along. "You created that?"

"Naturally." Devon smiled. "Brilliant, isn't it?"

"It's horrible!" Tristan stared at the other in shock. "It's only purpose is to destroy — everything!"

"Well, that's the *point* of a virus, isn't it?" Devon asked, sighing heavily. "My Doomsday Virus can wipe the Net out completely."

Tristan couldn't understand Devon; he didn't seem to comprehend what he was talking about. "But if you do that, people will *die*!" he protested. "And the entire world will suffer."

"Yes, of course." Devon rolled his eyes. "That's the entire *idea*, you dummy. When I play, I play to *win*."

"This isn't some sort of a game!" Tristan yelled. "This is *real*. People will be killed. Life will come to a halt. The whole planet will be reduced to chaos."

"You're starting to understand," Devon agreed. "People *always* die; I'm just nudging the statistics a bit. The only ones who'll perish are the losers, the weak, and the stupid." He shrugged. "About ninety percent of the human race, I'd guess. So who'll miss them?"

This double of Tristan's was a literal monster; he didn't seem to have any feelings whatsoever. "How can you talk about murdering billions of people as if it's just *fun*?"

"It *is* fun," Devon insisted. "It will be me, proving my superiority. I shall destroy *everything*. Once the Doomsday Virus is released, this stupid little planet will discover that I have the power to finish it off. And, once that's done, the survivors will have to come to me for anything that they want. I'll be the only one with working Terminals."

"You're sick," Tristan decided. "A monster. You can't do this. Think of all of the suffering it will cause!"

"Big deal." Devon smirked. "But if you want to talk about suffering, think about your own. I can't afford to have you around, Tristan. There's no way you could interfere with my plans, of course, but you're an obstacle in my path. I have to remove you."

"I already have interfered with your plans," Tristan said slowly. "I accidentally activated your virus."

"And there's the nub of the problem you present," Devon admitted. "Our DNA is identical, so you can get into everything I can. As a result, you have to die — and every last atom of your flesh must be disposed of. Can't afford to let anyone else get hold of your DNA." He smiled. "Nothing personal, of course, but — bye." The image reached out and tapped his speedboard.

The internal doors of the Connor house suddenly opened, though the outer ones remained locked. The lights came back on, allowing Tristan to see again. The windows were still polarized, and he was locked within his home.

"Did you hear about that poor family on the news in the Chicago area?" Devon's image asked. "Their home Terminal went crazy and flooded the house, thinking it was on fire." An alarm started to blare in the house. "Oops. Looks like the same thing's happening again, doesn't it? Must be a virus . . ."

Tristan knew he didn't have much time. The house sprinklers had already "detected" a fire, and water was hissing from them. He could hear the bath start up, too, pouring more water. He remembered the news item, and how everyone in that house had drowned. Devon was going to make the same thing happen to him now.

Unless he could stop it.

He dived for his computer, and tapped frantically on the speedboard. He didn't want to try voice commands, because that would alert Devon to his intentions. If only he could regain control of his Terminal from Devon in time . . .

"My, what a busy little bee you are," Devon mocked

him. "But it won't do you any good; I have complete control of your house."

"Oh, yeah?" Tristan fired off a command that let loose his guard dogs. Devon couldn't control what he didn't know about . . . he hoped! His Screen told him that a dozen of the dogs were loose, and they immediately started to attack Devon's link into the Terminal.

Water was creeping across the floor toward him. Tristan was already soaked from the sprinkler in his room, and his furniture was ruined. Luckily his Terminal was shockproof. But how much of this could it stand before it shorted out?

"Tricky," Devon murmured. His image bent over his own speedboard. "Your own little viruses, eh? Trying to cut me loose? Well, let's see how good they are. . . ."

Tristan hoped they were good enough. While Devon was distracted, battling off the guard dogs, Tristan set the program to multiple duplication. It would keep generating and releasing copies of his guard dogs until he stopped it. That should keep Devon busy. Then he ran the tracer program that he'd used to regain access to the Net. He needed to know how Devon had gained control of his Terminal.

The water in his room was a couple of centimeters or more deep now, and rising quickly. Tristan didn't know how much time he'd have before the power system shorted because of the water. Once it did, he'd be fried. What a great choice — drown or be electrocuted. He knew he didn't have very long before he'd face his death. Unless his plan worked.

Devon was occupied fighting off the guard dogs. This was buying time, all right; but would it work?

There were several hissing sounds from the direction of the kitchen. The appliances must be shorting out. It would be only a matter of minutes before his Terminal went dead, killing him in the process. *Come on, come on!*

The Screen lit up with the connection that Devon had used to gain access to the Connor house. Typing desperately, Tristan accessed the codes and disconnected it.

"What are you doi —" Devon asked, before his figure blinked out of existence. The sprinklers closed down and the windows turned clear again. Sunlight streamed into the soggy house.

Tristan grinned; he guessed he'd shown Devon which of them was cleverer now. But he couldn't stay here, that was obvious. Devon wouldn't give up this easily. Besides, the house was soaked, and the Terminal might short at any moment. Tristan gathered up his wrist-comp and raced for the door. He tapped in the code, and it started to open.

Devon's image reappeared in the room, looking out of the door.

"Did you think that was the trap?" he asked, highly amused. "Just kidding! I wanted to see how well you played the game. *This* is the real trap."

The door opened, and the three thugs were standing there, their tazers aimed at Tristan. His heart sank, and he was suddenly very afraid.

"Take him away, boys," Devon called to the men. "Kill him and incinerate his body."

The men stared at Tristan grimly. One gestured for him to come out. With no choice, Tristan obeyed. The flitter was standing in the road, waiting to take him to his death.

13

Genia was definitely thinking that she'd made a mistake going to the shields. Inspector Shimoda didn't seem to be very sympathetic, and Genia didn't like the way she was constantly threatening to send her to jail. As if she were just some common crook!

Still, the shield had a nice apartment and a really good Terminal. Genia wanted to try it out, but the inspector vetoed that idea immediately. Instead, she fed a small DNA sample into the scanner and had it checked out. While she was waiting for results, she brought some lemonade for the two of them. Genia wondered if this was the woman's idea of bonding. If so, she was dumber than she looked.

"Now what?" Genia asked, sipping the rather good drink.

"If what you claim is true," Shimoda said, "then I may be able to tag the virus and send it back to wherever it came from. I'll include a worm, and that will alert me to the source. Then I can have the creator arrested."

Genia frowned. "That's quite a sophisticated program you're suggesting. Are you sure you're up to it?"

"Quite sure," the inspector answered. "You're not the only computer-literate person in the world, you know."

Before Genia could say anything, the Terminal chimed. "The DNA sample matches that of Senior Vice President Borden," it announced.

"Damn," muttered Shimoda.

Genia scowled. "Isn't he one of the top guys at Control?" she demanded. "Why are you checking up on him? You think *he's* the traitor?"

"I don't know if he is or not," the inspector answered honestly. "And I wasn't aware that I was checking him to begin with. So the duty officer *didn't* switch the sample. But it's not possible . . . unless . . ."

"Somebody did what I do," Genia offered, intrigued

by the puzzle. "They snatched some of his DNA to access his accounts."

"No," Shimoda replied thoughtfully. "I saw the sample taken directly from a young man's skin. No, there's only one answer — a clone."

"A clone?" Genia was getting confused here. What did this have to do with a virus. "Isn't that illegal?"

"So is stealing," Shimoda pointed out. "But you do it."

"Point taken." Genia still didn't understand. "You think he's grown himself a clone?"

"I don't know," the inspector replied. "Maybe. Or maybe one was grown without his knowledge. Either way, it means that somebody else has access to everything that Computer Control knows. Whoever the bad guys are here, they know what we know. And that's not good news."

"So now what?" Genia just wanted this stopped so she could be safe again. Already, she had to figure out some way of getting her life back once this was done. She couldn't imagine that this shield would simply let her go.

"Now we try your virus." Shimoda sat at her Terminal and worked silently for about fifteen minutes. Genia watched and was honestly impressed with the other woman's skills. Shimoda had created a protective barrier to stop the virus from growing or infecting any system.

Then she wrote a command program that would force it to return to "home," wherever that was. Finally, she attached several worms to it. Only when that was done did she take Genia's chip and place it in her machine.

"Elegant work," Genia said.

The inspector nodded at the compliment. "Let's hope it works," she said. She hesitated a second, and then tapped in the final command.

Immediately, the virus was freed. If Shimoda had made a mistake, it would start to expand, eating up data, and reproducing out of control. The inspector had her finger ready to abort and isolate her computer so that the virus couldn't infect the Net. But nothing like that happened. Her security measures seized the virus and attacked it.

"It's working," Genia said, breathlessly, watching the status line. "You've got it captive. It won't ravage the Net."

Shimoda nodded, her eyes fixed on the Screen. "And there it goes," she said with satisfaction. "It's starting back to where it came from. Now all we have to do is to follow it . . ." She bent to her work. ". . . And then we've got our villain."

*   *   *

Devon felt a warm glow as he reflected on what he had done. With Tristan destroyed, he would be unique again. That threat was over. And it was Tristan who had prematurely released the Doomsday Virus. All the trails would lead to him. Devon would be secure.

How had the other boy come to be? And who had planned it? Was he Quietus's secret weapon, in case Devon had proven to be uncontrollable? It was possible, of course. Devon was so important to the group's work that they surely would never have taken a chance on only him. If he had turned against them, they would have been in serious trouble.

For the first time in his life, Devon felt alone. If Tristan was the Malefactor's creation, then Quietus had planned all along to have a weapon to use against Devon. They didn't trust him, and they were making sure that they were in a position to dispose of him. Alternatively, they didn't know about the cloning, and somebody else was involved in the game.

Which meant that the Malefactor and Quietus were being out-thought and out-fought. And that meant they were weak.

Either way — weakness or treachery — one thing was clear: It was time for Devon to cut himself free of them. He couldn't afford to stay with them any longer.

He no longer really needed them. *He* had the Doomsday Virus, after all, and he wasn't afraid to use it. The Malefactor was setting up his own plans to survive the virus, of course, and didn't want it released until he was ready.

Devon's fingers moved to his speedboard. But there was no longer any reason to bother with the Malefactor's schedule. Devon was ready *now*, and it would be the work of seconds to set the virus loose and watch the world come crashing down — and Quietus with it.

And, as soon as Tristan was dead, he'd be safe. . . .

The Terminal chimed. "The Doomsday Virus has been detected," it reported.

"What?" Devon whirled around to glare in disbelief at the screen. "Impossible! Nobody can access it!"

"It is not your virus," the Terminal explained. "Another party has released a controlled form of the virus into the Net."

It wasn't possible! Devon grabbed his keypad and started to trace the alarm. He realized in seconds that the Terminal was right. There was a virus fragment in the Net, heading back toward his station. A cold sweat broke out all over him as he realized what had happened. Someone had managed to isolate a strand of his virus, and had tagged it. Then they were sending it back, to track it and find him.

It had to be the authorities! How had they ever managed this? Devon was certain that they couldn't have done it. Still, just how they were doing it wasn't important. What mattered was to stop them, immediately.

He loosed his worms instantly, setting them after the virus fragment. But even as he did, he knew it wouldn't work. He'd designed the virus to be able to fight off anything like this. It had to be able to take out anything, otherwise it wouldn't do its job.

And that meant that he couldn't stop it.

In a matter of five minutes, the authorities would have his address and would be here to arrest him.

Devon couldn't let that happen. Not after all he had done so far. There *had* to be a way out.

The problem was, he could think of only one.

They couldn't track him down if the Net itself was purged. And there was just one way to do that. It would destroy *everything*, of course, but so what? Nobody else was important; only his security mattered. This intrusion had simply forced him to do what he'd been contemplating anyway. It was time to play his key move in The Game.

"Terminal!" he ordered, his mind made up. He could rebuild later as long as he escaped the authorities. "Release the Doomsday Virus. Immediately!"

"Released," the Terminal confirmed. It was only a machine, of course, and had no concept of what it had just done.

Devon stared at the Screen, which abruptly went blank.

The first of many . . .

The end of the world had arrived.

The virus leaped from Devon's holding area, hungry, strong, and unstoppable. It began to devour anything nearby, spreading as it went, accessing everything in its path.

New York began to shut down. The power systems started to die. Computers seized up. Everything came to a sudden, dead halt.

The world was ending in fits and starts.

"No . . ." whispered Shimoda, staring at her Terminal. She had been watching the progress of the viral strand as it backtracked its route. It must have been spotted somehow, because everything was going wrong. The Terminal was acting crazy.

Genia glanced up, clearly bored with the wait. She stiffened. "What's happening?" she asked.

Shimoda leaped to her feet and moved next to the

girl. They were looking out of her eighty-fifth story window, due south into the heart of New York.

Lights were dying out. Billboards went blank. Air conditioners shut down.

Shimoda's apartment died. The power went totally, cutting off her Screen and access to the Net. There was silence in the room, except their breathing, as they stared out on the city.

The pedways stopped below, throwing people into heaps. Shimoda winced; in her imagination she could hear the sound of breaking bones. Some bodies hit walls of buildings. Flitters stopped, throwing passengers into the road, leaving long, bloody smears as they slid away. In the air, several Newsbots simply stopped flying and crashed down to the sidewalks far, far below.

Genia gripped Shimoda's arm so tightly the inspector yelped. The girl pointed into the sky.

An aircraft heading toward Kennedy Spaceport seemed to have a fit in midair. It was only a few hundred meters from the ground, its engines racing. The pilot seemed to be having trouble with it, as the wing flaps opened and closed. Genia couldn't understand what was going on. Surely the plane's computers would correct even the worst mistakes of the pilot. That was what they were for.

Unless . . . they weren't working. . . .

The aircraft swept lower and lower. Genia watched, appalled and fascinated, as it shook and shivered in the air. Then one wing tip dipped, and the plane plunged. It was mere kilometers away from where she was standing when the lower wing caught on a tall building and ripped free. The wing burst into flames, as fuel lines severed, and caught fire from the sparks created by screeching metal. The wing ripped a chunk from the building, scattering blocks to the road below. The aircraft seemed to pause for a second in the air, and then folded in on itself. The other wing tore free, spewing fuel and fire across the houses nearby. Then, with a horrible roar that grew with each second, the body of the plane hit the ground. Metal howled, flames leaped, and the craft twisted and burned. Shockwaves pummelled the city.

Genia stood, unable to move, watching the plane crash and demolish houses in its path. It simply plowed through them, bringing them crashing to the ground. Hundreds of people died instantly. Horrified, transfixed, she watched the fireball grow and explode. Even at this distance, she felt the heat wash over her.

"It's the end of the world," Genia breathed.

"It's that virus," Shimoda informed her. "The maniac has released it! It's shutting down the whole city!"

Without power, there was absolutely nothing she or anyone else could do to stop it.

Tristan clenched his fists tightly, his palms slick with sweat. He was, to be honest, absolutely terrified. These three thugs were going to kill him and there was nothing that he could think of to stop them. He was reasonably athletic, but he couldn't possibly fight off three grown, trained men. Especially when they were armed.

But he wouldn't give in. He wouldn't just let them kill him. There had to be something that he could do. Some weakness to exploit . . .

The windows suddenly turned see-through again, and the driver swore. The flitter braked without warning. Tristan fell back against the door.

It gave way, and with a yell he rolled out. He hit grass, luckily, and managed to roll with the impact. His shoulder blazed with pain, but he managed to protect his head. Dizzily, he stared at the flitter.

It had lost all control, and carried on in a straight line, colliding with a light pole. The vehicle's metal screamed, the glass shattered, and it twisted and spun across the road, tumbling over and over.

It left three long streaks of red in the road, as the thugs were shredded in the crash. Tristan felt both sick and triumphant at the same time. He was glad he was safe, but he was ill watching men die.

Tristan managed to stagger to his feet. He was shaken, and bruised, with a small cut on his face. He'd been incredibly lucky, really. It was hard to focus his thoughts, but he tried to work out what was happening. He was still close to his home, by the look of things. He recognized the area from his infrequent walks. Nearby were neighborhood houses, tidy, quiet, self-contained, like his own.

As he looked, the power died in each of them. Lights flickered out, air conditioners stopped, and all sounds ceased. From a busy, humming street, the place had turned silent. Nothing was moving that required power.

He shook his head, trying to focus his thoughts. Why had the flitter malfunctioned like that? Why was the power dying? There was a reason, but it wouldn't quite come into focus.

Then he heard the sound of an explosion in the distance. A huge plume of fire was blazing into the sky. Smoke curled up, black and evil. And then came a second explosion, farther away. He shielded his eyes from the glare, unable to understand what was happening. Something was happening, something big. Something that could wipe out the power grid, and make — what?

factories? office buildings? — explode. But he was sure that in moments he'd hear the shrill sirens of the rescue trucks.

But there was nothing. Everything was still, save for the growing cloud of smoke and the smell of burning. Where was everyone?

Another explosion lit up the sky. What could possibly be causing this? It was like the end of the world, and nobody was doing anything about it.

And then he knew.

It was the Doomsday Virus. Devon had released it.

There would be no rescue workers to clean up, and to collect the wounded and the dead. There would be *nothing* but chaos and death.

The release of the virus had saved his life for the moment.

But the rest of the world was dying.

TO BE CONTINUED IN:

about the author

JOHN PEEL is the author of numerous best-selling novels for young adults. There are six books in his amazing Diadem series: *Book of Names, Book of Signs, Book of Magic, Book of Thunder, Book of Earth,* and *Book of Nightmares.* He is also the author of the classic fantasy novel *The Secret of Dragonhome,* as well as installments in the Star Trek, Are You Afraid of the Dark?, and The Outer Limits series.

   Mr. Peel currently lives just outside the New York Net, and will be 145 years old in the year 2099.